"I don't suppose you know anything about people shooting at eagles around here?" Jenna asked.

Keith shook his head. "Grandpa has a rifle, not a shotgun." He narrowed his eyes. "He wouldn't shoot at a bird anyway."

He seemed protective of his grandfather. She hadn't intended to accuse. "That means you have trespassers."

"Trespassers?" He rubbed the five-o'clock shadow on his jaw. "You mean other than you, Jenna Murphy?" His tone lightened; all the suspicion she had heard earlier was gone.

Jenna's breath caught. Something in the way he had said her name made her think he did remember her more than he was letting on. Was her perception of their friendship so much different than his? True, he had been two years older than she was, but she had felt such a special bond with him until that disastrous summer when he'd changed so much.

What had happened between then and now?

Books by Sharon Dunn

Steeple Hill Love Inspired Suspense

Dead Ringer
Night Prey

SHARON DUNN

has always loved writing, but didn't decide to write for publication until she was expecting her first baby. Pregnancy makes you do crazy things. Three kids, many articles and two mystery series later, she still hasn't found her sanity. Her books have won awards, including a Book of the Year award from American Christian Fiction Writers. She was also a finalist for an *RT Book Reviews* Inspirational Book of the Year award.

Sharon has performed in theater and church productions, gotten degrees in film production and history and worked for many years as a college tutor and instructor. Despite the fact that her résumé looks as if she couldn't decide what she wanted to be when she grew up, all the education and experience have played a part in helping her write good stories.

When she isn't writing or taking her kids to activities, she reads, plays board games and contemplates organizing her closet. In addition to her three kids, Sharon lives with her husband of twenty-two years, three cats and lots of dust bunnies. You can reach Sharon through her website at www.sharondunnbooks.com.

Night Prey

SHARON DUNN

Steeple Hill®

Published by Steeple Hill Books™

STEEPLE HILL BOOKS

Steeple
Hill®

ISBN-13: 978-0-373-67443-5

NIGHT PREY

Recycling programs
for this product may
not exist in your area.

PLEASE RECYCLE
THIS PRODUCT IS RECYCLABLE

He will cover you with his feathers,
and under his wings you will find refuge;
His faithfulness will be your shield and rampart.
—*Psalms* 91:4

A special thanks to Becky and Kyla for showing me around the local raptor rescue center and to all the dedicated people across the country who rescue and care for these awe-inspiring birds.

ONE

"What are you doing on this land?" The male voice pelted Jenna Murphy's back like a hard rain.

She dropped the empty pet carrier and raised her hands slowly, not wanting to spook whoever had called out to her. Most of the locals knew her, but a lot of strangers were moving in and buying ranches. If she had stumbled on an overzealous landowner with a rifle, the situation could get sticky. Her skills lay in soothing birds, not people.

"Please, I can explain." She struggled to get the words out, already winded from running up and down hills.

"Explain away." The silky smooth quality of the voice behind her did nothing to diminish the threatening tone.

Chances were, she was trespassing. When she got focused on something, she tended to space out everything else. Whose land had she wandered onto anyway? She'd been too busy trying to catch an injured hawk to notice if she had crossed boundaries. She had started her chase out on the King Ranch.

A glance at the mountain range to her left helped her orient herself. She was still on Norman and Etta King's ranch. Both of them were getting up in age. Maybe they had hired some help. The man's voice had a distant familiarity to it. If he wasn't barking orders, she might be able to place it.

His voice softened. "I didn't mean to scare you. You can put your hands down and turn around."

Jenna pivoted. She studied the man in front of her. He didn't have a gun. Instead he held a tool that was used for digging fence posts. His forehead glistened and the front of his shirt was stained with sweat. So the Kings *had* hired help...or had they? She looked closer.

"Keith? Is that you?"

Twelve years of her life fell away. He had changed quite a bit, but there was enough of the old Keith Roland for her to know this was her childhood friend and the Kings' grandson. The gray eyes that appeared blue in intense light were the same. "It's Jenna Murphy," she added when he didn't respond. "We used to play together when you spent summers with your grandparents, remember?"

The man standing in front of her bore little resemblance to the boy she had rafted the river with. Together, they had built a tree house that attracted a neighborhood of kids, summer after summer. His features were the same, though his muscular frame was a sharp contrast from the skinny kid she remembered. Keith's wavy brown hair now fell past his ears. The long-sleeved shirt he wore was a little out of place considering what a hot summer day it was. The almond shaped eyes still held the same gentleness, but something about this man seemed…haunted.

Keith blinked as if she had stunned him. He shook his head and furrowed his brow. "Sorry."

Did he really not remember her? Jenna's spirits sank. Funny, he had been such an important part of her childhood, the highlight of her summer. Yet, she hadn't even been a blip on his radar. Maybe she had just been the scraggly little tagalong kid to him. Somehow, she couldn't believe that. She touched her palm to her chest. "You almost gave me a heart attack when you shouted at me like that."

"I didn't mean to frighten you." His voice held

a warm quality. "We had a trespasser yesterday, too. I was concerned Gramps's place had become Grand Central Station."

Jenna laughed. Now she understood why he had been so quick to confront her. "That was probably me you saw. I'm the director of the Birds of Prey Rescue Center up Hillcrest Road." When she got a call on an injured bird, there usually wasn't time to inform landowners. All the locals knew if they saw her on their land, she was probably just taking care of a bird. She always dressed in bright colors, so she could be spotted from a distance.

"So that was you I saw tromping around yesterday when I was mending fence. Do you make a habit of trespassing?"

"The bird I rescued yesterday was an eagle with buckshot in her wing." Finding that bird flapping its flightless wings had broken her heart. Hopefully, she had gotten to the bird quickly enough to prevent infection but only time would tell. And now, she had an injured hawk to catch in the same area. It was unsettling to have two injuries occur so quickly. If someone was hurting her birds on purpose, she would get to the bottom of it. "I don't suppose you know anything about people using shotguns on eagles around here?"

Keith shook his head. "Gramps has a rifle, not a shotgun." He narrowed his eyes. "He wouldn't shoot at a bird anyway."

He seemed protective of his grandfather. She hadn't intended to accuse. "That means you have trespassers."

"Trespassers?" He rubbed the five o'clock shadow on his jaw. "You mean other than you, Jenna Murphy?" His tone lightened; all the suspicion she had heard earlier was gone.

Jenna's breath caught. Something in the way he had said her name made her think he remembered her more than he was letting on. But why had he tried to hide it? Was her perception of their friendship so much different than his? True, he had been two years older than her, but she had felt such a special bond with him until that disastrous summer when he had changed so much.

The last time she had seen Keith, he had been seventeen and deeply troubled. That was the summer his visit had ended abruptly with an arrest for drunk driving. Etta and Norman King had been heartbroken about sending their grandson away, but the arrest had been the final straw. Keith's drinking had led to wrecking farm equipment, nearly running over his grandfather and stealing from his grandparents. They had

had no choice. His wildness had put everyone at risk. Jenna shook off the memories and returned her focus to the task at hand.

"That eagle went down on your grandfather's property. Any idea who might be doing something like that?"

He drew his eyebrows together and his voice intensified. "No, but I will find out who it is. It's not right to do that to my grandparents."

Jenna turned her attention to the pet carrier she had dropped. "If you don't mind, I have an injured hawk to catch." She scanned the shorter trees and the undergrowth. No sign of the bird. The wounded hawk couldn't get airborne, but had managed to bounce for miles as she'd tried to chase him down. A flightless bird didn't stand much of a chance of survival. She had to find him before nightfall.

Jenna picked up the carrier and stalked a few feet away. She turned back around. "Good running into you, Keith Roland. I didn't think I'd ever see you again."

He lifted a chin in acknowledgment of her comment but offered nothing in return, no explanation of what he was doing in town or how long he planned to stay. He must have mended his relationship with his grandparents, but when? What had he been doing for the last twelve years?

Shortly after the summer Keith left, Etta King had run into Jenna in town. She'd shown Jenna a picture of a clean-cut soldier, Keith. Etta had expressed hope that enlistment in the marines would "straighten that boy out." Jenna didn't run into Etta very much, and talking about Keith was painful for both of them. She had no idea if the military had been good for Keith or not.

She strode a few feet up the hill.

"Do you need some help finding that bird, Jenna Murphy?" Keith shouted after her.

For someone who didn't remember her, he seemed to like saying her name.

A gust of wind wafted down the mountain, causing the limbs of the evergreens to creak. The breeze caught Jenna's long brown hair and plastered it against her face. She shoved the wayward strands behind her ears. "That would be nice."

After staking the post hole digger in the ground, he walked toward her with large even strides.

The wind settled. Something crashed in the forest, breaking branches. The injured hawk? No, it sounded like something bigger. Heavier. More dangerous. Jenna caught a flash of movement up the hill.

A noise she had never heard before shattered the silence. A sort of explosive snap pounded against her eardrums.

Keith's eyes grew wide. He leaped toward her. "Get down." He wrapped an arm around her, pulling her to the ground.

Her palms hit the hard earth; vibrations of pain surged up her arms. "What is going on?" She scrambled to get to her feet; he yanked her again down to the ground.

His arm went across her back like an iron bar. "We're being shot at. Stay down."

"Shot at?" Jenna shook her head in disbelief. Why would someone be shooting at them? Could it have anything to do with the injured birds?

Still on his stomach, Keith scanned the landscape around them.

A second popping explosion stirred up a poof of dirt five feet in front of them, confirming Keith's words.

Jenna's heart revved into overdrive. Her mouth went dry. "I've never been shot at before."

He put his lips close to her ear. "I have. I know what to do. Those rocks up there will give us some cover." He rose to a crouch, pulling her with him by grabbing the back of her shirt. "Stay low."

Jenna's mind reeled; she fought for a deep breath. What was happening? Why would anyone want to shoot at them?

Keith wrapped his arm around her waist. "You have to keep moving."

The strength of his voice in her ear freed her from the paralysis of panic. At least somebody knew how to respond.

Her heart pounded wildly. Keith dragged her up the mountain.

Another shot shattered the air around her. She screamed. She stumbled.

Keith pulled her to her feet. "Stay with me, Jenna."

She gasped for breath as he nearly carried her the remaining feet to the outcropping of boulders. Keith guided her in between two large rocks. The massive rocks allowed them both to crouch unseen and safe for the moment. Jenna pressed her back against the hard surface while Keith faced her.

Her pulse drummed in her ears. A tingling chill spread over her skin. She placed a hand on her somersaulting stomach. She could have died.

He touched a warm hand to her cheek. "You all right?"

Every muscle in her body trembled. "No. I'm

definitely not all right. Maybe you get shot at all the time, but I don't."

"Jenna, look at me and take a breath." He clamped his hands on her shoulders.

She shook her head, unable to focus. Her thoughts moved in a hundred directions at once.

His palms pressed against her cheeks forcing her to look at him. "You're safe here. You are out of the line of fire. Do you understand?"

The warmth of his touch and the steadiness of his gaze calmed her. She stared into the deep gray of his eyes. She nodded. Not only did he have experience with being shot at, obviously he had dealt with someone falling apart, too. As he had said, he knew what to do.

The forest fell silent. Keith scooted away from her and scanned the sky above them.

"Why...why would someone be shooting at us?" Her throat was parched. An intense craving for a cup of cool water overwhelmed her.

"I don't know, but they didn't do a very good job of it. Either they are really bad shots or they weren't aiming to kill. Maybe they are trying to scare us away." He leaned forward to see beyond the protection of the rocks.

"Be careful." She grabbed his arm, feeling the hardness of muscle beneath fabric.

"I don't see anything out there." He settled back, pulling his knees up to his chest. "We'll wait a while."

Their feet intertwined in the small space. Pebbles pricked the skin on Jenna's hand as she rested her palm on the ground.

"I wonder what the trespassers are doing on Gramps's land."

"You mean besides shooting at us…and shooting at eagles and maybe hawks, as well?" A shudder ran through her body. She pressed her feet harder into the ground in an effort to get beyond the trauma of what had happened. They would have to report this to the sheriff when they got out of here. *If* they got out of here.

Minutes ticked by. Her heart rate returned to normal. Searching for something to take her mind off the gunshots, she studied the man in front of her, looking for signs of the boy who had been her summertime friend. The scar over his left eyebrow was new. She wondered what other scars he carried. Had they made him want to forget his past? Maybe for him the pain of what had happened when he was seventeen overshadowed any of the positive memories. She had chosen to remember the good things about those summers.

"So where did you learn how to dodge bullets like that?"

Keith shifted his feet and looked away from her. "It's the second lesson they teach you in the marines."

"What is the first?"

"How to shoot them."

The vagueness of his answer and the icy tone indicated that he didn't want her probing. She stared down the hillside where she had left the cage intended for the hawk. With any luck, the bird hadn't gotten too far away.

Keith combed his fingers through his hair. "You think the people that just shot at us shot at your eagle?"

Jenna shrugged. "One eagle doesn't mean there is a pattern. I don't know what is going on with this hawk." She sucked in a breath as concern about the eagle ate at her stomach. Her vet friend had helped her dig out the buckshot. The female eagle, who she had named Greta, was on antibiotics. Hopefully, she would make it. But at least she was getting treatment. The hawk was still there on its own.

He rubbed at a spot of dirt on his worn jeans. "You take care of birds?"

"Just raptors, birds of prey. We rehab them and release them back into their habitat. I landed the job after I finished my degree in wildlife management."

He studied her for a moment. The corners of his mouth turned up. "You always did attract wild things."

Warmth pooled around her heart. "So you do remember me?"

"I remember you liked wild things. You were the only girl in town who thought feral cats made good pets."

Jenna lifted her chin. "All they need is love and for their food to be in the same place every day."

Keith laughed. A familiar twinkle returned to his eyes.

A connection sparked between them, and she leaned closer. "Is it all coming back now?" she teased.

The change in mood was short-lived. A veil descended over his eyes, and he pulled away from her. "You look different, that's all."

"People grow up. They change." How much had he changed over the years? Was he still battling the same demons that had driven him to drink at seventeen?

"Been quiet for a while. Maybe it's safe for us to head back down the mountain, huh?" He leaned out, glancing from side to side.

Her heartbeat sped up as fear returned at the thought of leaving their safe haven. Her stomach clenched as she wrestled with her choice. Part of her just wanted to leave, but she knew a flightless bird didn't stand a chance. He would starve or be eaten if she didn't catch him. If only Keith would stay with her. It wouldn't be so frightening if she wasn't alone.

A shrill cry pierced the forest.

"The hawk," she whispered.

Keith pushed himself to his feet. He studied her for a moment. "So how hard is it to catch a wild bird?"

Relief spread through her. He had all but read her mind. "Not hard at all if I have help," she gushed. Shielding herself behind the boulder, she eased to her feet. "But we need to catch him soon. He might be able to survive on bugs for a while but some creature is bound to decide he looks like a delicious main course before nightfall."

"I can't leave you out here considering what just happened." He rolled his eyes theatrically. "So I guess that means I have to help you."

She scooted toward him and smiled. "I guess so."

Keith stared at the petite, slim woman standing in front of him, her dimple showing as she smiled. One thing for sure hadn't changed about Jenna Murphy. She was as cheerfully determined as ever when it came to rescuing wild animals. "We need to be cautious."

Anxiety flashed over her features, but then she squared her shoulders as if summoning courage. "I know. Let's go get the cage. With two of us, he shouldn't take any time at all. We can surround him."

Keith squinted, studying the mountain and forest. The shots had come from uphill. He suspected a long range rifle had been used. The knowledge that the shooter was far away didn't make him any less vigilant.

A slight breeze bent the boughs of the pines. He didn't detect any movement that might be human. "Okay, but be ready to drop to the ground if you hear anything." He could handle being shot at, but the thought of anything happening to Jenna didn't sit well with him.

Jenna ran down the hill and picked up the cage. Keith trailed behind her, assessing the landscape for any movement or sound that was out of place. He stayed close, so if he had to, he could pull her to the ground quickly. Her reflexes weren't as fine-tuned as his, which meant he'd have to be doubly vigilant to protect her. And he *would* protect her.

Of course, he remembered her. Over the years, she had come to mind more than once, but he had always pushed those memories down to some hidden place, not wanting to visit the bittersweet emotions that came with remembering.

Seeing her again had shocked him. Jenna was a bright girl who could have done anything with her life. He had always assumed she would move away from the small town of Hope Creek. He never thought he would see her again. Memories threatened to swamp him now, but he refused to let himself get distracted.

Keith remained tuned in to the forest, watching the trees and listening.

Out of breath, she came up to him. "The last time I saw the little guy he was headed in that direction." She pointed to a stand of lodgepole pine.

"What's the game plan here?"

Jenna pulled a cloth from her back pocket. "If we can get a covering on his head, it will calm him. Then I can get him in the cage for transport to the center." She untied the silk scarf around her neck. "You'll have to use this."

He nodded. "Let's get this done so you and the bird can get somewhere safe. And then maybe next time you can forego the trespassing."

"I have to make the birds my priority. There

is not always time to inform the landowner. Everyone around here knows me." Strength had returned to her voice.

Keith clenched his jaw. When Jenna got an idea in her head, she was like a pit bull. She just wouldn't let go. "We need to be careful up here from now on, Jenna, even if it was just teenagers being stupid with guns this time." He hoped that's all it was. That was bad enough. His grandparents were older and vulnerable. He didn't like the idea of some town kid taking advantage of that.

"I'll be careful, but this is serious. Someone shot at that eagle on your grandparents' land. That is against the law." Her voice, fused with emotion, broke. "I don't like it when people hurt the birds. I won't know what's going on with that hawk until I can get a look at him. What if someone has been shooting at him, too?" She turned and stalked up the hill.

The scent of Jenna's perfume lingered on the scarf she had given him. He held it for a moment before putting it in his front pocket as he followed her uphill. It would be so easy to get caught up in the whirlwind of Jenna Murphy trying to save all the wild animals. Twelve years ago, the house where Jenna and her father had lived had been a menagerie of the songbirds her father took care of and all the unwanted and injured animals Jenna had adopted. He smiled at the memory.

She stopped and turned to face him. "If you don't want me tromping on your grandfather's land, you can come with me each time." Her tone was playful.

Heat swept up Keith's face. She was standing so close. "I've got a lot of work to do for my grandfather." His heart hammered in his chest. Did she have any idea what kind of effect she had on him, even after twelve years?

Jenna pivoted. "I saw movement over there." She craned her neck. "That's the hawk." With the cage banging against her thigh, she darted toward the trees.

Keith followed behind. She stopped abruptly on the edge of a clearing. He peered over her shoulder and saw a medium-size bird with gray-brown feathers. Jenna stepped back and slipped behind a tree, pulling Keith with her. He towered over her by at least ten inches. She stood on tiptoe and pulled his head toward her to whisper in his ear.

"He hasn't seen us. If you circle around to the other side, we have double the chance of getting him. Wait for a moment when you have a clean shot to throw the cloth on his head, and I'll do the same. Whoever gets to him first, the other person needs to move in quickly."

His heartbeat sped up when she stood this close. Her breath made his ear hot. Twelve years ago, he had just begun to see her as a young woman and not a buddy. The feelings that had barely blossomed before she rejected him were still as strong as ever.

After squeezing her shoulder to indicate he understood, he slipped into the evergreens, careful not to step on any underbrush. He knew plenty about moving silently through the woods. He had trained for cold weather combat and then they sent him to the desert. Sometimes, the military didn't make any sense. He walked until he estimated that he was positioned opposite Jenna. He edged closer toward the clearing, still using the trees for cover.

A gust of wind blew through the trees. The hawk hopped off a log to the ground. The bird cocked his head and flapped his wings before settling. Almost indiscernible movement on the other side of the clearing told him where Jenna was. The bird fluttered as though alarmed and turned so he was facing Keith. Jenna materialized in the clearing and tossed the cloth over the bird. In a flurry of movement, Keith dove in. His vision filled with feathers and a sharp object pierced his hand. He swallowed a groan of pain.

When he oriented himself, Jenna had secured the cloth on the bird's head with a piece of leather. Her fingers wrapped around the animal's feet.

Blood oozed from the cut on his hand as the pain radiated up his arm. He followed Jenna to where she had set the cage.

Jenna made soothing sounds as she slipped the now still bird into the cage and secured the door. Her voice was like a lullaby. She turned to face Keith. A gasp escaped her lips as she grabbed his hand. "You're bleeding."

He pulled away, tugging the cuff of his shirt so it covered his wrist. "It's all right. I can take care of it." He didn't want her looking at his arms.

"I should have warned you—their talons are like knives."

"So I discovered." Keith held out his uninjured hand for the cage. "I can take that."

They hiked toward Jenna's Subaru with the sun low on the horizon and the sky just starting to turn gray and pink. His old Dodge truck was farther down the road.

"Thanks for helping me," Jenna said. "I always thought we worked together pretty well."

Flashes of memory, of kayaking and rock climbing with Jenna, surfaced. They had had fun together. "We didn't work. We played."

"Still, we were a good team."

Keith studied Jenna's wide brown eyes. Being with her opened too many doors to the past and the painful memory of her turning her back on him when he had needed her most.

A muffled mechanical sound caused them both to stop in their tracks. In the distance, just beyond the rocks where they had taken cover, a helicopter rose into view. The machine angled to one side moving away from them.

Jenna's expression indicated fear. "Tell me your grandfather has recently purchased a helicopter."

Keith shook his head.

Jenna's fingers dug into his upper arm. Her voice trembled. "Do you still believe this is just foolish kids with firearms?"

TWO

Jenna placed some live grasshoppers in the rescued hawk's cage. Though the sense of panic had subsided, she still felt stirred up by what had happened. She tried to calm her nerves by focusing on doing routine things around the rescue center. She could deal with anything a wild bird did, but being shot at was an entirely different story. The hawk picked hungrily at the food. Except for the occasional beating of wings, the rescue center was quiet this time of night. All the volunteers and the one other staff person had gone home.

Outside, she heard Keith's truck start up. Their encounter with the helicopter and being used for target practice had left her feeling vulnerable. When Keith had seen how shaken she was, he'd offered to follow her in his truck to the rescue center.

She had phoned Sheriff Douglas and told him

about the helicopter and being shot at on the King Ranch on the drive home. Even then, as she retold the events to the sheriff, it had been a comfort to look in the rearview mirror and see Keith following her.

She didn't know what to think about Keith Roland. He seemed like a different person from the one he'd been that last summer, but the memory of his destructive teenage behavior made her cautious. And there was no denying he was more distant now. She thought of how he had jerked away when she'd tried to pull back the cuff on his shirt to check the wound from the hawk's talons. But he still was able to make her feel safe. She wouldn't have had the courage to get the hawk without his help.

She grabbed a torn sheet and safety pins from a bottom shelf where medical supplies were stored. As she pinned the sheet onto the cage, the beating of wings and scratching sounds slowed and then stopped altogether. She'd done an initial exam but couldn't find a reason why the rescued hawk couldn't fly. It had been a relief not to find any sign that this bird had been shot. Both dark and pale mottling on the bird's breast and flanks indicated that he was a fairly immature Swainson's hawk. She had a theory about this bird. Flying was part instinct and part learned skill.

In the morning when her assistant Cassidy came in, they'd be able to do an X-ray to make sure there was no physiological reason the bird was flightless. Cassidy was on call 24/7, but Jenna had decided that the bird had been traumatized enough for one day. The X-ray would go better once the bird was hydrated and had his strength back. And Jenna would do a better job after a good night's rest let her shake off the last of her jitters. Maybe by morning the sheriff would call with a perfectly logical explanation for the gunshots and helicopter…and even if he didn't, it would be easier to feel brave in the daylight. For now, she'd just finish up things at the center and head home—hoping that her hands would stop trembling somewhere along the way.

Jenna checked on the bald eagle she had found yesterday, Greta. They had done an X-ray to make sure they'd gotten all the buckshot but that didn't mean the bird was out of the woods yet. Infection from the wound was still a concern. The eagle didn't react when Jenna looked in on her. She was still weak.

Jenna skirted the area that housed the cages filled with smaller birds and stepped into the office. An owl sat on a perch by her desk. She made clicking noises at Freddy, who responded by stepping side to side on his perch. Freddy was one of the center's permanent residents, who served as an ambassador bird when Jenna did her presentations to schools and groups. Only the birds who would die if released in the wild got to stay at the center on a long-term basis. Freddy had fallen out of his nest and been rescued by a boy. The bird had imprinted on humans. As an owlet, Freddy thought he was a person. He was capable of flight but probably wouldn't last long in the wild.

Jenna filed through the stack of papers on her desk. There was still work to do, but she could do some of it from her house, located just behind the center. She grabbed the camera from a drawer. She had a bunch of photos she needed to transfer to her laptop for the center's newsletter. Once she had everything she needed to take home with her, she stepped out the back door into the cool evening of late summer. The flight barn to her right and a separate building up the hill that housed the other ambassador birds were silhouetted against the night sky, and she smiled at the sight of them. She loved the world she'd built for herself and her birds—and she wouldn't let anyone harm it.

Her feet padded on the stone path to her house. The cool breeze caressed her skin, and a handful of stars spread out above her. God had done some nice artwork tonight. Late summer in Montana was her favorite time of year. The center stayed busy, and the weather was perfect. Jenna opened the door and stepped inside her living room. She left the door open to allow the evening breeze to air out the stuffy house.

After retrieving the computer cord for her camera from a kitchen drawer, she shifted a stack of magazines and bills she had piled on her coffee table and flipped open her laptop. The wallpaper on her desktop was of an eagle perched on a tree. Now that people had been shot at, the sheriff seemed more concerned.

He had been dismissive yesterday when she had called him about the eagle. He had theorized that the bird had been in the wrong place at the wrong time and had been shot by accident. She had reported the incident to the game warden, as well, who had expressed a little more concern. She didn't expect everyone to be as upset about injured birds as she was, but shooting at eagles was illegal even if they weren't on the endangered species list anymore. Jenna shuddered. She cared about the birds, but after what had happened today, going out into the forest alone would be no easy task.

She wasn't going to let herself get hopeful. In her experience, poachers were almost impossible to catch unless they were discovered with the dead animal or there were witnesses. Because Greta had been injured with a shotgun, there was no bullet to trace.

Knowing Sheriff Douglas, his looking into the events on the King Ranch would probably not happen until the next afternoon. Finding out who had shot the eagle was probably even lower on his priority list, and she doubted he was giving any weight to her theory that the two shootings might be related—that someone could be targeting the birds.

A crashing noise emanated from inside the rescue center. Jenna jumped to her feet. What on earth was going on? She ran through the open door and raced up the stone path. The sound had come from the side where the birds were housed. Jenna pushed open the back door, and gasped.

The sheets had been torn off all five of the cages. A golden eagle fluttered and bashed itself against the wooden bars. A red-tailed hawk let out its distinctive cry, like a baby's scream. Medical equipment and the X-ray table had been pushed over. Two small Kestrel hawks flew wildly around the room, making high pitched noises that indicated agitation.

Jenna stepped toward one of the cages, then knelt and picked up the torn fabric that had covered it. Twisting the cloth, she turned a quick half circle. Fear spread through her. It looked like someone had gone through and randomly tossed off the cage covers to stir up the birds. It didn't look like any of the birds had been hurt, but they *had* been spooked, and so had she.

She shook her head as her mind raced. Who would do such a thing? And why? And most frightening of all—was the person still there?

The sharp slap of one object slamming against another startled her. It had come from the office. Her heart pounded. Someone was in the next room. She wished she could call for help—she had the sudden memory of Keith from before, sheltering and protecting her—but her house had the only land line. They used cell phones for the center, and her cell was in the Subaru.

Grabbing a pair of surgical scissors for a weapon, she pushed open the door that separated the birds' cages from the office area. She scanned the room. Freddy's perch had been knocked over. That must have been the noise she heard. Freddy might have been alarmed and pushed it over himself…or someone could have knocked it over. Her eyes darted from the top of a low file cabinet to her desk, Freddy's other favorite places to perch.

"Freddy?"

Her stomach twisted into a knot. If someone had hurt or stolen that little bird… She checked several more places before finding Freddy backed into a corner behind an empty bucket. Poor little guy. After settling Freddy again on his perch, she surveyed the rest of the room. Her breath caught. The front door was slightly ajar. Someone had been in the office, too. She raced across the room, slammed the door shut and dead bolted it. Then she grabbed the keys off a hook and exited the rear door, careful to lock it behind her. Was the intruder still around? She was going to have to call the sheriff right now. Her feet pounded the stone walkway. She glanced from side to side. She'd have to check on the birds in the other buildings and clear up the mess the vandals had made later.

By the time she burst through the open door to her house, her legs were wobbly. Her sweating hand fumbled with the lock, and then she turned her attention to the phone. She had just heard the dial tone when she noticed her laptop had been turned around. She walked over to the coffee table and stared at the screen. The photograph of a bird had been replaced by a message.

STAY OFF THE KING RANCH OR THE BIRDS
IN THE CENTER WILL DIE, ONE BY ONE.

Keith lifted the cover off the painting he had been working on and dipped his brush in a shade of blue he thought would capture the intensity of the Montana sky. He clicked on a light and positioned it so it shone on the canvas. This attic room in Gramps's house, which he had set up as his living space, was hardly an ideal artist's studio. It had small windows. At this hour, there wasn't any natural light at all. Lack of ventilation made the space hot in the evening. But even with all its flaws, he liked the place for the quiet it provided.

In the corner of the sparsely furnished space, a German shepherd rested on a bed. With only a little brown on his nose and at the ends of his paws, Jet was an appropriate name for the therapy dog the V.A. had provided.

Keith took in a deep breath. It had to be past midnight. He slept on an erratic schedule and when he couldn't sleep, he painted. Originally, his physical therapist had prescribed painting as a way of getting his dexterity back, but the hobby had proven to be useful for working out emotions, as well.

Seeing Jenna again had stirred him up. Had it been a mistake to come back here? After the death of his mother, it had seemed as though God was leading him back to the ranch to heal things between him and his grandparents since they were his only living relatives. Now he wasn't so sure.

Grandma and Gramps had long ago turned off the evening news and gone to bed. They had adjusted to their night owl in the attic. The arrangement seemed to be working out well. The attic had a separate entrance with outside stairs, so he could come and go without bothering them. He helped out as much as they would let him. In the two weeks since he had been here, he and Gramps had mended some fence and repaired the dilapidated barn. He had tiled an entryway for his grandmother and weeded her garden. It felt good to make amends for what had happened twelve years ago, and they had welcomed him back with open arms.

The summer he had his first drink, a fellow kayaker who had been like a father to him had drowned on a run that Keith had decided not to go on at the last minute. Keith had spent a week in turmoil wondering if he would have been able to save his friend if he'd been there. At seventeen, he hadn't known why he'd started drinking. Only when he was in treatment did he realize the alcohol numbed the guilt and confusion. His brush swirled across the canvas. In the left-hand corner, he'd painted an eagle in flight. He'd done that before he had ever run into Jenna Murphy. Jenna with the bright brown eyes. Jenna who had been a skinny-legged ten-year-old the first time he had seen her sitting in the park reading a book. Jenna who had become a beautiful woman.

He angled away from the easel and massaged his chest where it had grown tight. He had kept all those memories behind some closed door. Whenever he allowed the good memories in, the bad ones were bound to follow.

The last time he had seen her, she had been fifteen, standing with her back pressed against the door of her house. The silence of the summer night had surrounded them as she looked up at him. That night, he'd come to her house for a reason. He hadn't expected her cold response.

"Keith, I heard about what you have been doing…about the drinking."

"I haven't had anything to drink for a week." She had refused to be a part of his drinking life, so they hadn't seen each other for two weeks.

The time apart made him realize how much she meant to him. His grandparents' lectures hadn't stopped his craving for alcohol, but he'd quit for Jenna…if she'd help him. He didn't want to lose her.

"I know about all the bad things you did. Everyone is talking." Her voice held a desperate pleading quality. "You're my friend, but we—we can't stay friends if you're going to act this way."

"I'm trying to change here, Jenna. I have changed." He pressed the heels of his hands against his forehead. "I know this summer has been a mistake."

Her lips pressed together, disbelief evident in her features, like she didn't have any faith in him. Didn't she know who he really was?

"Jenna, I've realized something. That's why I came here tonight. To talk to you. To tell you I don't want to be just your friend." He leaned toward her, close enough to be enveloped by her floral perfume. "Please."

She studied him for a long moment. She turned her head away. "You need to go. You're scaring me." Her voice fused with fear.

He had seen his life as being at a crossroads that night. He was looking for a safe harbor to escape the destructive storm he had created.

Her friendship had always been a stabilizing force in his life. After two weeks apart, he had thought maybe he knew what she meant to him. He had gone there with plans to kiss her for the first time, to let her see how important she was, how badly he needed her help. Apparently, the friendship had just been about fun to her. She hadn't been willing to listen to him or weather the challenge he faced. Her rejection had propelled him back to his drinking buddies.

Though he had been angry at the time, he took responsibility for the arrest that had happened later that night. Looking back, he was glad it had happened. It had been a wake-up call. When his legal entanglements had been addressed, he enlisted. By the time he was finished with boot camp, he had gotten help and sobered up.

But the way Jenna had abruptly and completely cut him out of her life was what he could not get past. She hadn't come to see him in jail and wouldn't come to the phone when he'd called to say goodbye, as if all five summers together were washed away by one month of bad choices. She didn't stick around long enough to see that he had changed.

The image of her turning her head to one side was as vivid as if it had happened yesterday. Keith clenched his jaw. He squeezed out more blue paint on the palette. His brush made broad, intense strokes across the canvas.

If Jenna hadn't cut him out of her life, things would have been different. They would have stayed in touch. She would have known he'd gotten his act together shortly after that night.

Though the death of his friend had triggered his drinking, the emptiness of never having known his father had laid the foundation. If AA had taught him anything, he knew he couldn't blame Jenna for his life choices. But still, he had been vulnerable with her, revealed his true feelings. And he had been rejected. He would never put himself in a place where she could hurt him like that again.

He had dated other women in the twelve years since he'd left Hope Creek in disgrace. Some had broken up with him and he had ended other relationships, but nothing had hurt as much as her turning away from him that night.

He flexed his fingers to try to work out the ache in them. Even though he had stripped down to his T-shirt, the attic space was still hot. He collapsed in a chair and stared at the work he had done so far. It was an okay landscape, but nothing that threatened Charlie Russell's reputation.

Apparently sensing Keith's distress, Jet rose

from the bed and padded over to his owner. He rested his head on Keith's leg, licked his chops and let out a sympathetic whine. Keith stroked Jet's smooth, soft head, the movement drawing his attention to his wrist.

He ran his fingers along the braided scar that started there and moved up the inside of his arm to the crook of his elbow. He had an identical scar on the other arm, only not as far up. Scars on his chest, as well, showed where the power of the blast had embedded debris.

His life had changed in an instant by a roadside bomb. Both arms had been blown apart by the explosion. The speed at which they had moved him off the battlefield and a skillful surgeon had saved his life and his arms. He had lost some strength and dexterity and the scars would be there forever. But he thanked God every day that he was alive.

He didn't realize it at the time, but God had brought a father replacement into his life in the form of a caring drill sergeant, who helped him find his sobriety while still in boot camp. But it wasn't until his tour in Iraq and the accident that his understanding of God had changed. When he was in rehab staring at a hospital ceiling, he had found the faith that his grandparents had modeled summer after summer. Like his grandfather, he didn't talk much about his faith, though he felt it deeply.

Keith wiped the sweat from his brow and stared at the eagle soaring in the immense painted sky. Despite his attempts to forget, he did remember Jenna; and now every detail of their summers together came at him like a flood. He hadn't thought he would ever see her again. He had assumed she would leave for college and never come back. There was nothing to keep her in this dinky town. Her mom had died when she was two and though she'd been close to her father, the man had always encouraged her to follow her dreams.

He had come back to Hope Creek for two reasons: to make amends to his grandparents for the damage he had done when he was seventeen, and for the solitude. Iraq had been more than he had bargained for. He needed time to sort through his life and find his bearings again. Jenna hadn't been on the agenda. How was it possible that with all that had happened, the dormant attraction could be revived just by seeing her?

Keith rose to his feet and picked up his brush. Maybe he should just paint over that eagle. He stood back to examine his work. No, the bird looked right flying up there in the huge sky. He dipped the tip of his brush in the blue and mixed it with white.

Someone rapped gently on the outside door. Who on earth would be knocking at this hour? Keith's chest tightened. Maybe there had been an emergency with Gramps or Grandma.

He grabbed his long-sleeved shirt and raced over to the door.

When the door swung open, Keith's jaw dropped, and he took a step back. "Jenna. What are you doing here?"

THREE

Keith's reaction to the sight of her was a lot calmer than she had expected, considering the hour. He seemed surprised, but not displeased to see her. Even though he was barefoot, it didn't look like he had been sleeping. Streaks of paint decorated the thighs of his faded jeans. His brow glistened with sweat, yet he wore a long-sleeved shirt.

"Someone broke into the center…and into my house. They left this note on the computer." The trembling in her hands made the sheet waver.

Keith took the piece of paper she'd printed out.

"I know it's late, but I thought you should see that." Jenna's legs were still wobbly, and her stomach had tied itself into knots. Right now, it didn't feel like she would ever eat again.

Keith read the note. His expression hardened. "Did you tell the sheriff?"

"Both him and his deputy are over there right now. They let me go after I answered their questions. They could see I was upset, and they asked me if there was anyone who..."

He reached out and brushed a hand over her cheek. "You don't look so good. Do you want to come inside?"

Like breath on a window, the warmth of Keith's touch faded slowly. He was the first person she'd thought of when the fear over the vandalism had overwhelmed her. Even if the incident didn't involve the King Ranch, she would have craved his calming influence. As though a day hadn't passed, she had slipped into the old patterns of their relationship.

Though she was curious about where he lived, it was enough of an imposition to show up at this hour. "I don't need to come inside. Sorry to bother you this late. I just thought you should know, since it concerns your grandparents' place."

He relaxed his posture and leaned against the door frame. "How did you know I was up here?"

"It was the only part of the house with lights on." Her hand fluttered to her neck, where her pulse was racing. She hadn't calmed down even after the drive over. Whoever had broken into the raptor center and her house had succeeded in their attempt to scare her by threatening to harm the birds at the center. She was furious at the threat, but she was also scared. Very, very scared.

Keith ran his hands through his wavy brown hair, then slapped the note with his hand. "Don't tell my grandparents." Strength returned to his voice, and he lifted his head. "Grandma and Gramps shouldn't have to deal with something like this."

"Good thing you are here to help." The protective stance he had taken toward his grandparents was admirable. She found herself wishing he had been at the center earlier. He would have known what to do with the intruder. Maybe if Keith had stayed awhile to visit, there wouldn't have been a break-in at all. Though she tried not to, mental images of birds fluttering wildly and the note on her laptop made her legs wobbly all over again.

Keith stepped toward her. "You look kind of pale. Are you sure you don't want to come in and sit down?"

Jenna stepped across the threshold. "It's kinda hot in here."

"Not much ventilation," he said.

She moved back outside and turned on the

tiny landing. "I think the cool night air would be the best thing for me." She was surprised that after all these years, he was still keenly tuned in to her emotional state. Surprised and flattered.

They had learned to read each other while rock climbing the last summer they were together. As climbers, they had always gone out in a group, but Jenna had proved to be his best climbing partner. Keith had been mentored by an older climber the year before. The next summer, their last summer together, he had taught Jenna. Because their lives depended on it, they had become adept at knowing not only what their climbing partner would do physically while hanging from a cliff face, but how their emotional states affected them. She wondered what he was reading from her now. She felt so anxious and confused, she didn't know what to do. But his presence was making it better.

She stared up at the sky. Pulsating stars and wispy clouds accented the black dome above her. Strength returned to her limbs. She wasn't shaking anymore.

Keith rested his back against the railing, lacing his hands together over his lean stomach. He looked up. "It is peaceful out here, isn't it?"

"Always calms me down." She took in a deep

breath of fresh night air. "Better than therapy."
She bent her head, tracing the dark outline of
the jagged mountains and flat buttes against the
lighter shade of sky. Off in the distance, a light
blipped and disappeared. She pushed herself off
the railing. "What was that?"

Keith leaned toward her. "What?"

"Over there by those buttes. I think I saw
a light." She squinted and took a step toward
the opposite railing, cupping her hands over
the rough wood of the two-by-four. "I'm pretty
sure I saw something. Do you have a pair of
binoculars?"

"I can find some." Keith stepped into the huge
room, opened a couple of bureau drawers and
lifted a coat and sweater as Jenna peered inside.
Artificial light gave the space a warm glow. The
place was free of clutter. Keith seemed to desire
a bare bones existence. A black German shepherd settled in the corner.

She took a step inside. "I didn't know you
had a dog." The shepherd lifted his head but
remained in the bed.

Keith opened a cupboard. A dorm-size refrig-
erator and double burner resting on counter
space indicated that the area functioned as a
mini kitchen. "That's my buddy, Jet."

Jenna took another step inside. Two paintings,

both landscapes, caught her eye. They were places she knew well, a river and a mountaintop no more than a few miles away. Was Keith aware that he was painting their childhood haunts?

"Found them." Keith pulled a pair of binoculars from a lower cupboard.

She retreated to the balcony and turned her attention back to the area where she had spotted the light. Nothing caught her eye. Still, she couldn't shake the feeling that something or someone was out there.

Keith's bare feet padded lightly on the wood floor. Once outside, he handed her the binoculars.

She leaned toward him and pulled the binoculars up to her face. She adjusted focus and scanned the landscape filled with shadows. "I saw what looked like a glowing light."

Keith surveyed the tiny landing and then looked up. "Maybe if we get higher." He tested the railing by shaking it. "I'll climb first and then pull you up."

He jumped on the railing and flipped himself on the roof with the deftness of an Olympic gymnast. He turned and stared down at her. "Your turn."

Already, her heart was racing. As a young girl she had had a fear of heights. Keith had helped her overcome that, but she was out of practice. The old fears were back. She handed him the binoculars first and then crawled on the railing. "This brings back some memories."

"We never climbed houses." There was something guarded about the statement.

"Just rock cliffs, right?" Her life would have gone on a completely different trajectory if she hadn't met Keith when she was ten. Like her father, who was the town's librarian, she'd spent most of her time with her face buried in a book. She had always loved nature, but Keith's desire to teach her to kayak and climb had awakened her sense of adventure. If it hadn't been for him, she probably would have ended up working in a lab somewhere instead of running the rescue center. And she definitely wouldn't be here, about to climb on the roof of a house, looking for answers to a mystery.

"You're going to have to stand on that railing," he coaxed.

"I know." Her hands were sweating.

Keith pushed himself to the edge of the roof. "My hand is right here."

She eased to her feet, finding her balance by resting a hand on the wall. Whether showing her how to rock climb or build a campfire, he'd been a patient teacher. Jenna lifted her head and locked into Keith's gaze. She reached for him. He gripped her wrist. The warmth of his touch permeated her skin to the marrow. "I'm dizzy."

"I'm right here. Other hand. Let go of the wall, Jenna," he soothed.

He pulled her up and into his arms in one easy movement. She scooted toward him and away from the edge of the roof. Her hand rested on his chest. Beneath the softness of the cotton shirt, his heart pounded out a raging beat. She bent her head, out of breath. "I never did learn to like heights." The truth was that when she was hanging from a mountain, if it had been anyone else beside Keith holding the rope, she probably wouldn't have been able to climb.

"You always did just fine." His voice warmed.

His face was close enough for her to hear the soft intake and exhale of air. She could smell his soapy cleanness. She'd kept Keith Roland frozen in time. All these years, he'd been the boy who was her summertime buddy. But he wasn't a boy anymore. His transition into manhood had been marked by such tragedy that she'd held on to the part of him that had been so wonderful, the boy part of him. Here in front of her, holding her, was the man she couldn't make heads or tails of.

He scooted away, and the coolness of the night enveloped her. "Let's see if we can spot anything from here," he said, clearing his throat.

Jenna pulled her knees up to her chest. Then she studied the outline of the mountains. Again, a light flickered and disappeared. She pointed and grabbed his arm. "Right about there."

He lifted the binoculars, craning his neck slowly.

"See anything?"

He shook his head. "Maybe if we stand."

"On the roof?"

He laughed, and there was something of the adventurous boy in the laughter. "Come on, you know I can talk you into almost anything."

"That was when I was twelve. This is not a mountain. We don't have any ropes to catch our fall. *You* stand up."

He nodded. "Suit yourself." He handed her the binoculars and eased himself to his feet. His hand reached down, brushing the top of her head while he continued to look straight ahead. She grabbed his hand at the wrist and placed the binoculars in them.

He wobbled as he lifted them to his face but maintained his balance. Jenna held her breath. She tilted her head.

"I see them," he said a moment later. "Lights…

moving." After putting the strap around his neck, he let the binoculars fall against his chest.

"What could it be?"

"People on my grandfather's land." His voice intensified. "It's hard to tell exactly where they are at this distance. Gramps and I used to ride all over the place on dirt bikes, but it's been a while since then. I don't know the trails as well as I used to."

"I've gotten pretty good at reading the landscape from having to rescue birds in the weirdest places."

"That would involve you having to stand up," he teased.

She took in a breath. "I can do it."

"That's my brave girl."

Her heart lurched. That was what he used to say to her when she made the decision to do something, even if it scared her.

He extended a hand to her and she rose to her feet. She leaned against him to steady herself. She could see the front edge of the roof from here. Even before she straightened her legs, the night sky was spinning around her. She dug her fingers into his arm. He braced her by placing his arm around her waist.

"Steady," he whispered in her ear.

His hair brushed against her cheek. "Ready

now?" She nodded, and he brought the binoculars up to her eyes. The view through the lens was not spinning. Pulsating circles of light floated phantomlike across the landscape. She could discern another larger stationary glow. "Somebody is definitely out there."

"But where are they exactly? Gramps's place is thousands of acres."

She moved the binoculars across the view in front of her. The outline of the mountains revealed the shape of a wizard's hat and a formation that everyone called the Angel's Wings. "They have got to be close to Leveridge Canyon."

"I remember that area. Should we call the sheriff, tell him where to go?"

Jenna shook her head. "The sheriff's still looking for fingerprints at my place. It would take him a while to get over here. We should go out there now before they leave. What if what is going on out there now is connected to the shooting and the note?"

He rubbed his hands on his jeans, angling his head away from her.

"Someone is trespassing on your grandfather's land. We can find out who is doing this and turn them in," she persisted. If they caught whoever was doing this, they wouldn't be able to harm the birds at the center.

The thought of any kind of confrontation terrified her, though. She needed Keith's help. Why was he hesitating? The events of the afternoon showed that he could handle himself just fine, better than she could. "Please Keith, I can't do this alone."

He crossed his arms and stared out at some unknown object as though he were mulling over options. He turned toward her. "I don't want you going out there by yourself. It could be dangerous."

"Thank you."

He shook his head and let his arms fall to his side. "I'll see if I can find a map that might help us pinpoint where they are. The dirt bikes are fueled and ready to go in the garage."

In less than fifteen minutes, they had climbed down from the roof and run to the garage. Jenna placed the bike helmet on her head. She watched him buckle a gun belt around his waist. Considering what had happened this afternoon, the gun was a reasonable precaution. Still, her heartbeat quickened as she slipped on her bike gloves. What were they riding out to?

Jenna turned the petcock on the fuel tank, choked the engine, flipped out the kickstart.

Without a word, Keith sauntered over to her bike while she stepped aside. He jumped down on the kick start. The engine revved to life. She had never been able to get a bike started on the first try.

While Keith started his own bike, Jenna swung a leg over the worn seat. She twisted the throttle to a high idle.

Keith burst out of the barn on his bike. Jenna clicked on her headlight and sped out after him. He waited for her on the road. The hum and *putt putt* sound of the bike motor surrounded her as she caught up with him, and they headed toward the dark horizon.

FOUR

The helmet enveloped Keith's head, pressing on his ears and creating an insulated sensation. He glanced back, taking note of the soft glow of Jenna's headlight. Despite the rough terrain, she kept up pretty well. Part of him wished he could leave her behind and check out the danger on his own. He didn't want to put her at risk. But he doubted she'd let him go without her, and he wasn't about to let her go into the canyon by herself. Even after all these years, he felt the need to protect her.

Still, the pinprick to his heart, the memory of her rejection, had made him hesitate. When he had held her in his arms on the roof, her hand on his chest had seared through him. It had taken every ounce of strength he had to pull away.

At seventeen, he had just begun to see Jenna as a young woman. He had been clumsy and unsure of himself. His attraction for her came out through roughhousing and verbal jousts. When they were on the roof, her touch had been like breath on a glowing ember. He clenched his jaw. He revved the throttle on the bike and lurched forward. So what if the feelings were still there, stronger than ever? That didn't mean he had to do anything about the attraction and be hurt by her all over again.

The road narrowed. The bike bounced over the rocks. Up ahead, he could see the dark shadows of the granite boulders that formed the opening to Leveridge Canyon. He stopped the bike and flipped up his visor. The smooth hum of Jenna's bike growing closer filled the night air. The crescent moon hung just above the flat-topped buttes in the distance.

Jenna came beside him, geared down the dirt bike and flipped up her visor.

Keith pointed. "If we go this way, we can get pretty far into the canyon before we have to hike in."

She nodded. "Sounds good," she shouted as she revved up the bike motor. She flipped down her visor and sped off, kicking up dirt.

He closed the distance between them and rode beside her. She nodded in his direction and then sped a little ahead. Finally, she brought the bike to a stop and dismounted. Keith caught up with her, stopped his bike and pushed the kick stand down.

Jenna pulled off her helmet, gathered up her long hair and twisted it into some kind of knot that held it off her face. He had never quite figured out how she did that. Moonlight washed over her tanned skin accentuating the melting curves of her neck.

She hung the helmet on the handlebars.

Keith turned away. His forearms had begun to hurt from shifting gears and managing the bike over uneven terrain. "You probably ride all the time." He massaged the area above his wrist. Frustration shot through him. He just wanted to be able to do the things he used to do and not have to be reminded of his injury.

"Bikes do come in handy for work sometimes. Only when I try to start one, it takes three or four tries. It was nice to have help this time."

He detected a tone of gratitude in her voice.

She turned off the headlight on her motorcycle and took in a deep breath. "Tell me we have a flashlight."

"Why? You scared of the dark?" he teased as he clicked off his headlight.

"I'm not scared. You're the big chicken," she said.

He picked up on the strain in her voice. They

were joking because they were both nervous about what they might find in the canyon.

Sitting in the darkness, he said a quick prayer that he would be able to keep Jenna safe. His calm returned.

He loved the remote parts of the ranch far away from houses and any artificial light. The intensity of the darkness had always caused his heart to beat faster. Tonight, the surrounding vastness reminded him of how huge God was. He was just a speck in the universe and God loved him anyway.

"I'm not afraid, are you?" she challenged and then laughed at their game. Her boots scraped the hard rock. She moved so she was standing next to him. Her shoulder brushed against his, sending a charge of electricity up his arm. "It's like a game of chicken, right?" she whispered.

They stood for a moment, shoulders pressed together. The game helped lighten the tension over what they might be facing in the canyon. Keith focused on the gentle inhale and exhale of Jenna's breathing.

He leaned forward and felt along the handlebars until he touched the canvas tool bag, then reached in. His fingers wrapped around the cold metal cylinder of the flashlight. He clicked on the light and shone it in her direction being careful not to shine it directly in her eyes.

"Should we get going?" She turned and headed into the canyon.

Once she wasn't looking at him, he touched the gun on his hip. He had every confidence all his training meant he could deal with whatever they faced, but could Jenna? Once again, he thought that maybe he should have told her to go back home. But he knew he wouldn't have been able to talk her out of coming. Her determination to end the threat against her birds was strong. That somebody thought his grandparents' land was open for public use was wearing on him, too. The sooner they got to the bottom of this, the better.

He increased his pace and caught up with Jenna. He tuned into the sounds around him, ready to respond to any threat.

He shone the flashlight ahead of her. "Careful, you don't want to fall."

"I'll be fine," she said.

They hiked over the rocky ground as the canyon walls closed in on them.

She stopped and grabbed his wrist. "You hear that?" She spoke in a harsh whisper.

Keith turned his head and listened. A faint mechanical thrum, like a bee buzzing under a glass jar, pressed on his ears. He shone the light. Only the granite walls of the canyon came into view.

Jenna rested a hand on his shoulder. "We must be close. I say we keep going."

He picked up on a hint of fear in her voice. "Let me stay in front." He trudged forward, and she followed behind him. The noise faded in and out, but always sounded far away. The canyon walls, though, had a way of creating echoes that played tricks with sound.

The smolder of wood burning thickened the air and filled his nostrils. They were close.

The distance between the walls of the canyon increased as they stepped into an open flat spot with no vegetation.

He shone the flashlight which revealed motor-cycle and four-wheeler tracks. "What happened here?"

"Trespassers, big-time." Anger coursed through Keith. The nerve of people disrespecting his grandparents like this.

Jenna grabbed his hand and aimed the flash-light toward the source of the smoke. "It looks like the campfire was just put out." She walked over to it and kicked at the rocks that formed a circle.

Keith edged toward Jenna. "We could hear the

sound of their bikes on the way up the canyon. They are probably still pretty close."

Even though he couldn't hear anything now, an inner instinct told him they were not safe. The air felt stirred up.

He shone the light around the edges of the camp. Only blackness. A coyote howled in the distance. Jenna gripped his arm. Keith aimed the flashlight a few feet from the fire, revealing empty beer bottles. He wanted to believe that it was just teenagers having a party, but something felt more sinister here.

"Where do you suppose they went?"

He stepped away from the fire. The tire tracks went around in circles like someone was joyriding.

She continued to hold his arm as they stepped toward the surrounding forest. Some of the tracks led out of the camp to the east and others went in the opposite direction. "They split up," she said.

Or maybe not. It was hard to tell. The tire impressions were distorted by darkness and uneven ground. The riders had crisscrossed over each other's paths a dozen times.

As if she had read his mind, Jenna said, "I count two four-wheelers and two, maybe three dirt bikes."

"At least." It was a big group, anyway. He turned his attention in the other direction. Maybe another three or four riders had gone that way. What were they after? What had brought them here?

Jenna gripped his arm even tighter. "That's a lot of people," she said.

Whether they were teenagers or not, the thought of someone tromping around his grandfather's ranch and shooting at him and Jenna infuriated him. Had Gramps's land been targeted because he was older and less able to fight back?

Jenna tensed. "They're coming back." Panic filled her voice.

The mechanical clang of a bike motor echoed through the canyon. "I can't tell where it's coming from." Keith angled his torso to one side and then pivoted in the opposite direction.

The noise grew louder, then softer, then increased in volume again.

"This way." He wrapped an arm around her shoulder and stepped toward a stand of trees. After Jenna slipped behind a tree, he clicked off the flashlight and settled beside her on the ground.

The roar of the bike intensified. A second motor was added to the mix. He brushed a hand over the gun in his holster. Jenna pressed close to him.

They crouched with the darkness surrounding them. Jenna's clothes rustled as she shifted on the ground. She stiffened when the bike noise got louder and then relaxed when the clatter of the motors faded.

"I think they are gone," she said as she melted against him.

"Maybe." He couldn't hear anything, either, but he wasn't convinced the danger was over.

He clicked on the flashlight to have a quick look. Jenna uttered a sound as though she were about to say something. But then her fingers gripped his upper arm.

The roar of a four-wheeler was on top of them with the suddenness of an explosion.

Jenna stood up halfway, and Keith pulled her down as he clicked off the light. "You'll be seen."

In an instant, a four-wheeler was in the camp, followed by a second one, blocking the path Keith and Jenna had taken into the canyon. As the noise assaulted his ears, adrenaline surged through him. They couldn't leave the way they had come. Jenna clung to him, wrapping her arm through his.

The riders wore helmets, making it impossible

to tell who they were. One of the four-wheelers turned in their direction, catching them in the headlights. They'd been spotted. Keith turned, pulling Jenna deeper into the trees.

The rider turned off his engine and dismounted from the bike. He stalked toward the trees where they had taken cover.

Keith searched his memory for the layout of this part of the ranch as they ran through the forest. Behind them, one of the four-wheelers faded in the distance.

They scrambled through the darkness. A branch whacked against his forehead. He shone the light briefly to find the path with the least hazards and then turned it off.

Jenna tugged on his shirt. "This way." She sucked in air and struggled to speak. "We can circle back around to the other side of the canyon."

Behind them, branches broke and cracked. They were being chased.

Still holding on to Jenna, he plunged into the inky darkness. They worked their way down a rocky incline away from the trees. Keith glanced behind them where a light bobbed.

Out of breath, he whispered in her ear. "We need cover." He directed her back toward the forest.

After ten minutes, he stopped, leaning over and resting his hands on his knees. He took in heaving gusts of air. Jenna leaned against a tree, tilting her head. He slowed his own breathing so he could listen. Maybe they had lost their pursuer. He couldn't hear anyone behind them, but better safe than sorry.

He signaled for them to keep going. She fell in step behind him, resting her hand on the middle of his back to keep track of him in the dark. Their pace slowed, which allowed them to be more quiet. The forest thinned. Keith turned on the light. The landscape ahead looked familiar. They weren't far from the bikes.

Jenna came alongside. Her breathing had evened out.

They made their way across the rocky landscape. Keith kept his ears tuned to the area around them. Their feet caused an occasional stone to roll and crash against another.

Jenna planted her feet. "Where are the bikes?"

Keith clicked on the light and swept across the area where the bikes should be. The bikes were there, but they had been knocked over. He ran to the first bike and lifted it off the ground. After four tries, it started.

He helped Jenna get her bike up, but repeated

attempts at starting didn't even produce a choking sound. Keith lifted his head. The rider who left must have come down here to sabotage their bikes. It was a trap, meant to delay them. And it was working.

Jenna pointed from the control cluster across the handlebars. "It looks…looks like they pulled out these wires." She tried to ignore the rising panic.

"They must have run out of time before they could do that to mine."

"So they…they just pushed yours over."

The trauma of what they had been through was getting to her. Keith leaned close. "You doing okay?"

Jenna tilted her head to look into his eyes. His attentiveness helped her shake off the impending panic. "I'll make it. None of this seems to have ruffled your feathers."

"I've had more practice."

"You mean with the military?"

He angled away from her, picking up his helmet off the ground. "There is no electricity getting to the starter on that bike. You'll have to ride with me."

Just like that, he changed the subject. There were walls between them now that hadn't been there when they were kids. He seemed guarded about sharing any part of himself. What had he been doing for the last twelve years?

Keith got onto the functioning dirt bike and scooted forward, making room for her. Jenna put on her helmet and swung her leg over the bike. She sat up straight and placed her palms delicately on Keith's sides. Being this close to him made her feel even more light-headed and breathless than being chased down the canyon.

Keith flipped up his visor and turned his head toward her. "You can move closer. I don't bite."

"I'm okay." The smoldering tone of his voice made her heart race. At the same time, a fear seeped into her consciousness. She really didn't know anything about him, who he had become. The memory of the night of his arrest charged through her with full force. He had come to her for help. She had been afraid then, too, afraid that his turn toward delinquency would destroy her new and fragile faith. Her friends at church had told her to stay away from him. He could talk her into almost anything. She did not want to be pulled into that world. Not when she already knew how badly it could hurt.

The bike jerked across the uneven path

heading up an incline. Jenna slipped back on the seat, nearly falling off. She wrapped her arms around Keith's waist to stay on. His gloved hand patted hers. They lurched down the mountain until the path grew smoother.

He pulled onto a dirt road and increased his speed. Jenna glanced behind her. She couldn't see any headlights, but that didn't mean they weren't being followed. She held on even tighter to Keith, pressing against his back. Keith angled the bike into a curve. Despite the fact that he was a risk taker, she was sure he knew his limits. In all their cross-country treks as kids, he had never wrecked a bike. True, he was a daredevil, always had been, but there was something measured and calculating in every daring thing he did. She was safe on this bike. The only thing that had ever scared her about Keith had been the drinking.

Keith's wavy hair stuck out from beneath the helmet. She was tempted to touch the soft curls. She rested her chin against his shoulder as her eyelids grew heavy. The muffled rumble of the dirt bike motor surrounded her. Her arms relaxed. She closed her eyes and rested, still aware of the movement of the bike. When Keith leaned into a curve, she leaned with him.

He brought the bike to a stop by the farmhouse. The sky had turned from black to gray. Still enveloped in the insulating bubble the ride had created, Jenna sat up straighter. She pulled her arms free of Keith, slipped off the bike and flipped up the visor. Cool morning air surrounded her.

Keith flipped up his visor. "One of us is going to have to call the sheriff."

"I can do that. He's probably not at the center anymore." Their encounter in the canyon and being chased loomed in her mind, but the ride, being close to Keith, had made her less fearful.

Keith slipped off his helmet and ruffled his wild hair. "I don't know what to think about all this. I just know we have to put a stop to it."

"If we *can* put a stop to it." Her anxiety returned.

He stepped off the bike. "If all that has been happening is connected, it's too elaborate to be just teenagers."

She couldn't think about this right now. It was all too much. "I have to get back to the center." She wasn't looking forward to dealing with the aftermath of the break-in and the sheriff scouring for evidence. It had been a long night. Maybe she could catch a nap before she had to start another day. She shoved the helmet toward his stomach. "Thanks for the ride."

"At least that part of the night was okay, huh?"

Jenna looked into Keith's almond-shaped gray eyes. She found herself wanting to get to know him better, which meant that even after all the years and all that had transpired, she still liked him.

"Jenna?" His eyes searched hers. The intensity of his gaze electrified the air between them. He turned his chin toward his shoulder, shifted the helmet in his hand and said, "That was a good ride."

Somehow she had a feeling that was not what he had intended to say. "I'll tell the sheriff what we found. I don't know if it has anything to do with the shooting, the helicopter and the threat on my computer or not."

"I think it does." He lingered, kicking the dirt with his motorcycle boot. "I'll let you know if I find out anything."

"Let me give you my cell number." Even before she had finished her sentence, she knew she was looking for an excuse to see him again. She had to stop this. She couldn't hope for even a friendship with someone who was all closed doors and guarded secrets.

"I'll get a pen." He bolted up the stairs to his place, but stopped halfway.

Jenna drew her attention to where he was looking. She halted at the base of the stairs. Her breath caught in her throat. A red smear across Norman and Etta's door spelled out the word. STOP.

A chill seeped through her skin as Jenna struggled to form the words. "Is that…is that blood?"

FIVE

Sheriff Douglas raised an eyebrow when he saw Keith enter the station. No surprise there. Christopher Douglas had been a young deputy twelve years ago when Keith had caused so much trouble. Keith couldn't erase the prejudice some people in town had against him. In a way, he understood it. All he could do was show them that through his actions he had changed. But whether the sheriff believed that or not, Keith needed him to take this seriously.

The blood on the door had been the final straw for Jenna. Even though she put on a strong facade, he could tell she was rattled. Keith had decided to drive Jenna to the sheriff's office. No doubt, the men they had seen in the canyon had left the bloody warning. This was escalating fast, which only made his desire to get to the bottom of it even stronger.

The sheriff rolled his chair a few inches away from his desk. "Hello there, Jenna...and Keith."

Keith held out a hand. "Sheriff."

"Is this about the trouble up at Norman and Etta's place yesterday?" The sheriff's chair squeaked when he moved it back and stood up to shake Keith's hand. "I'm headed out that way later today. Or did you want to talk about the break-in at the center, Jenna?"

"I'm afraid that things have gotten worse rather than better." Keith filled the sheriff in on what they had seen in the canyon, and what had awaited them back at the house. He held up a baggie that contained a cloth with some of the blood on it. "Not only did we find evidence of trespassing, this was used to write a warning across my grandparents' door."

The sheriff tugged on his mustache before picking up the baggie. He opened it, took out the cloth and sniffed. "I'll have my deputy take a look at the door when we go out."

"Actually, we scrubbed it clean. I didn't want to upset my grandparents any more than I had to. We thought the blood sample would be enough."

"You won't be able to file vandalism charges. All the same, this might be helpful." The sheriff rested the bloody cloth in the plastic bag in his open palm. "I'll send it up to the state crime lab. Gonna take a while to process it. Nobody has reported a shooting. No one came into the emergency room."

"I was thinking it was from an animal...not a person. Maybe an eagle." Jenna shuddered. Keith placed a supportive hand on her back.

"Could be." Sheriff Douglas set the blood sample down on his desk.

"Did you find anything at my place last night?" Jenna asked.

The sheriff laced his thick fingers together. "My deputy and I went all over the center and your house. Place is like a crime scene nightmare. Lots of fingerprints and lots of footprints. We dusted your laptop and only found one set of prints, which is probably yours."

Jenna crossed her arms. "So that was an exercise in futility." Her voice swelled with frustration.

The sheriff held up a hand as if to stop her escalating emotion. "One thing concerned me. The way you described things happening made me think one person couldn't move that fast from your office to your house. My deputy and I reenacted what you said happened. We think one person distracted you with the mess in the center while somebody else was leaving the note on your computer."

Jenna's face blanched. Fear flashed across

her features. "Two people." The pulse in her neck became visible. "In my house. And in the center."

Keith leaned toward her. If it was that easy to break in, Jenna was not safe at the center. "Do you have a security system?"

She rested her palm against her forehead. "We're a nonprofit. It's on our wish list right after more cages and medicine." Her voice trembled.

This was upsetting her. He had to get her out of here. He spoke to the sheriff. "We'll stay in touch. I'll inform my grandparents you are coming out there. You don't need to tell them about the door, but they need to know about the trespassers. Call us if you find anything." He put light pressure on her back and guided her toward the door.

Once outside, Jenna crumpled as though she had been punched in the stomach. "I was okay last night, but now…" Her hand fluttered to her neck and she laughed nervously. "It…it just kind of hit me all of a sudden. A least two people were in my house, touching my stuff and disturbing the birds at the center." Her voice faltered.

Keith hadn't seen the layout of the whole rescue center, but she was vulnerable there living by herself if she didn't have a security system. "I suppose a watchdog is out of the question."

"You mean your dog. He'd freak out the birds." She combed her hands through her long hair, something she always did when she was anxious.

Her face still didn't have any color. He had to get her mind off this. "Look, neither one of us has had any sleep or food. I can solve one of those problems. What say I buy you breakfast?"

Jenna took in a deep breath and visibly relaxed. "Hunger might be part of what's making me feel so shaky. My stomach is growling." She pointed up the street. "Nora's Corner is open at this hour."

They walked the nearly empty street past the library. Even though the windows of the library were dark, Jenna's shoulder jerked when she looked in that direction. Her jawline tensed.

"Your father still work there?"

"Last I heard." Her words were clipped.

"So I take it you don't see him very much?"

"Can we please leave my father out of any discussion?"

Keith opened the café door for Jenna, who gave him a dark look. "I see him when I need to see him."

The café hadn't changed much in twelve years. The blue checked curtains looked new. If memory served, they used to be yellow. The Formica tables and vinyl covered chairs were the same, just a little more worn. The scent of bacon and maple syrup hung in the air. A plus-size blonde waitress looked up from the newspaper she was reading at the counter.

"Take a seat anywhere. Be with you in just a minute." The waitress grabbed the coffee pot and refreshed the cup of the only other customer, an old man wearing a baseball hat hunched over the counter.

Pots and pans banged and something sizzled on the grill in the half-visible kitchen. Country music spilled from a radio.

Jenna chose a table by the window. She glowered at him when he took a seat opposite her.

The waitress set two menus down on the table. "The blueberry pancakes are especially good today." She drew out her pad from the front of her apron. "They come with your choice of bacon or sausage."

"That sounds good. With sausage." Keith pushed the menu toward the waitress.

Jenna's lips flattened and her forehead creased. She opened the menu. "I think I would like to see what else is available." The waitress nodded and slipped away to give her more time. Jenna held up the menu, clearly using it as a barrier against him. Why was she so angry that he'd asked about her father?

If Jenna had chosen to stay around Hope Creek when she could have gone anywhere in the world, it must be because she still desired some kind of contact with her father. There was nothing else that would have kept her in town other than the need to be close to Richard Murphy, who had raised Jenna alone.

Jenna had been a free spirit, running around town in the early morning hours and late into the evening. At noon on the dot, though, she dropped everything she was doing and raced to the library to eat lunch with her father. Keith had gone with her a few times. He had envied the lively conversation between father and daughter as they discussed whatever book they were reading together. What had happened to spoil that? He wanted to know, but she obviously didn't want to tell him.

"What looks good to you?" he asked, hoping to change the subject.

Jenna didn't respond. She lifted the menu even higher so it covered all of her face. He reached across the table and slowly pulled the menu down. The wounded look in her eyes nearly knocked him from his chair. He'd struck a nerve. He needed to back off about her father.

He offered her a faint smile. "If I remember correctly, you liked cold pizza for breakfast."

She hunched her shoulders. "I don't think that is on the menu."

"Guess you'll have to settle for French toast."

"My second favorite thing." A faint smile brightened her face, revealing the dimples. She put the menu down and leaned toward him. "You remembered."

He was starting to think there was very little he had forgotten about her. He'd buried the details about her in some deep place, but her preferences in food, what she'd said and done on each adventure, the way she tilted her head to one side when she was thinking, it was all there. During the school year when he lived with his mom, he had had girlfriends. There had been women after he had enlisted. But he would be hard-pressed to recall much about them beyond their names.

The color had returned to her cheeks. Her long brown hair fell softly around her heart-shaped face. He rested his elbows on the table and leaned toward her.

The waitress returned. "Have you folks decided?"

She looked up from the menu. "I think I will be daring and have the blueberry pancakes."

"With sausage?"

"Bacon," she said.

He raised a teasing eyebrow. "Always got to be different, don't you, Jenna Murphy?"

Jenna's heart fluttered at how easy it was for them to fall into their familiar banter. A lot of things were easy with Keith. The waitress walked away from the table.

Keith tossed a sugar packet at her and she zinged it back across the table. "So you think the sheriff will figure out what is going on up there?"

"He'll do his best." The tension eased from Jenna's muscles when she realized Keith wasn't going to bring up the subject of her father again. "What do you think it is about, all those men and motorcycles and four-wheelers? Maybe some kind of smuggling?"

Keith shrugged. "A lot of drugs come into Montana from Canada."

The waitress brought their meals along with the pot of tea they had ordered. Jenna hadn't realized how hungry she was until she took the first bite of pancakes slathered with maple syrup. Her mouth watered. Both of them ate quickly.

Keith shoved the final piece of sausage in his mouth. "Come on, it's been a long night for both of us."

Jenna checked her watch. "The center will be opening in an hour." She'd just have to go without sleep.

Keith opened the truck door for Jenna, and she slipped into the passenger seat. He eased onto the two-lane road looking straight ahead. She studied his profile. The prominent nose and the angled cheekbones had always made him appealing, but now there was something weathered and wise in his demeanor that hadn't ever been there before.

He turned to look at her. "What?"

Her cheeks warmed. He'd caught her staring. "Nothing, just keep your eyes on the road, all right, buddy?" She said with feigned bossiness. His gray eyes held a depth and a knowing that was different. She turned away and stared out the window as the fields and forests clipped by.

She was glad he had dropped the questions about her father.

Except to make sure he was alive, she hadn't spoken to her father since the emergency room trip a year ago. It had been an awakening for her and the letting go of a secret that she had kept for so many years.

Her father drank. When she lived at home, the drinking began at night after he got home from work while he took care of his birds, so Jenna stayed away. In the morning, he hated himself for drinking so much, so Jenna left the house early to avoid his bad mood. Lunch at the library had given her a brief window of solace. She had her warm and intelligent father back. If the library wasn't too busy, they would sit in the soft chairs by the window, their feet touching while they both read. From time to time, one of them would read a passage out loud that they found funny or original.

As a kid, she had kept the secret without ever asking herself why. Maybe she had wanted to maintain her father's respectability. Embarrassment had been a factor. She'd feared too that the authorities might step in and separate her from her only parent.

She had started to see what a normal life was like when she moved away to college and didn't have to deal with her father's craziness every day. Then she had come back home, and the trip to the emergency room had been the final straw that told her things needed to change.

The emergency room people probably weren't gossips, but they had seen the damage Richard

Murphy had done to himself over the years. That someone else knew the secret had given her the strength to find help for herself, to confront her father and tell him that she couldn't handle it anymore. Fine if he wanted to keep drinking, but it hurt too much to watch him slowly kill himself. Richard Murphy was never angry or abusive when he drank, he was just sad.

Keith pulled onto the gravel lane that led to the center. He focused on the road, arms relaxed as he drove. Guilt had risen up in her when he had asked her about her father. Maybe it wasn't right to limit contact. She had wanted to tell Keith, to explain, but she hadn't been able to. Sharing this part of herself was still new and never easy. It was even harder with Keith, since her fear of him becoming an alcoholic like her father was what had caused her to turn away from him all those years ago.

Her eyelids felt heavy. She rested her head against the window. He brushed a hand over her hair with a touch as delicate as butterfly wings. Even though the road was gravel, Keith drove so the car didn't jostle very much. The fog of sleepiness filled her brain.

She felt the car come to a stop and heard Keith

talking to Cassidy through the open window, but the heaviness of fatigue made her awareness fade in and out.

Her car door opened.

"Come on, sleepyhead."

Her eyes burst open. His face was inches from hers. Keith smelled like the air after a cleansing rain. They were at her house.

"Keith, I have work to do." Her voice lacked commitment.

"I've already taken care of that." He held an arm out for her. "You're not going to be much good to anyone anyway until you have had a couple hours sleep."

She stepped toward him. He supported her by wrapping an arm around her waist. "You haven't had any sleep, either. You don't seem tired. Is that some kind of military trick?"

His body tensed. "Something like that."

More vague answers. They were both keeping secrets.

He led her down the stone path. When they got to her door, he held up a key. "I got it from Cassidy. She is the only other person that has a key, right?"

"Some of the volunteers have keys to the center, but not to my house."

"You might want to collect those...con-sidering."

Jenna shivered, considering that someone had promised to hurt her birds and was capable of breaking in. "All the volunteers are good people."

"That might be true, but you don't know who they know, who has access to their keys." He unlocked her door and pushed it open.

She trudged in. Her limbs felt weighted. "Okay, I am just going to take a nap and then I will get up. Can you tell Cassidy to come and get me if we have any calls to go out on? I don't want her to have to handle those alone."

"It's been taken care of, Jenna." The warm tone of his words comforted her.

She turned to look at him. Even in the ragged cotton shirt and the paint-stained jeans, he was good-looking. Not to mention strong and capable. If he said everything was taken care of, she'd believe him. "Thank you."

"I'll lock the door behind me and give the key back to Cassidy." He gazed at her. A softness entered his eyes. "Okay?" His voice had gotten husky with emotion.

So much was going unsaid between them.

The look on his face caused a zing of electricity through her. "Okay." She fought to keep the rising emotion out of her own voice. Almost immediately an ache entered her heart where a single look from Keith had made her feel alive.

Jenna opened the door to her bedroom. She could hear Keith walking across the floor and fumbling with the lock as she took off her shoes and lifted her fluffy comforter. She slipped into bed with her clothes still on.

She liked the idea of renewing a friendship with Keith, but it couldn't go beyond that. It didn't matter how nice Keith was. It didn't matter that even after all these years, they seemed to mesh so easily.

Jenna adjusted the pillow under her head as the soft comfort of down molded around her. She knew enough from the psychology rule book and her own dating history that she was attracted to men who in one way or another had the same destructive behavior as her father.

The night he had come to her door twelve years ago, she had wanted to keep her father's secret from Keith. She had been following the advice of friends to cut him out of her life.

And, on some unconscious level, she must have known that Keith would only hurt her like her father had.

Keith did seem different, but he had a bad track record. She couldn't take the risk to her heart.

SIX

Jenna awoke with a start. Had the noise she heard been a part of her dreams or an actual sound? She slipped from beneath the warmth of the comforter, planted her feet on the carpet and rose out of bed. When she pulled back the curtain, it was still light out. She checked her watch, nearly five o'clock. She had slept a full eight hours. Cassidy would have gone home by now. Jenna stepped into her loafers.

She felt a sense of urgency she didn't understand. She needed to check on the birds.

She grabbed her keys off the counter and headed out the door. Her first stop was the flight barn. The barn was designed to help rehabbed birds practice flying in a safe environment. It was over a hundred yards long with perches scattered around the front of the barn. The flight barn was their newest building, only a year old, courtesy of rancher Peter Hickman's generous fundraising. Jenna suspected that Peter had chosen to help the center as a way of becoming a part of the community that was slow to accept outsiders, but in any case, his annual fundraiser was an answer to prayer.

When she pushed on the sliding door to the flight barn, a golden eagle flew by her. The flapping of wings so close always caused her heart to race faster. The golden drifted to the ground at the far end of the barn, the brown feathers catching the light and revealing the gold sheen that was the reason for the eagle's name. Two other birds, a red-tailed hawk and another golden, walked on the ledges around the windows, occasionally fluttering their wings and doing short, quick flights.

She loved these birds, but she knew that in a way, her choosing to pour her energy into saving the raptors was a form of rebellion against her father. Her father had loved the less volatile songbirds, the domesticated ones and the wild, injured ones people brought to him to take care of. She'd gone for the fiercer, stronger birds, less prey to the kind of weakness her father had shown.

All the birds in the flight barn were present and accounted for. Still, something in her felt unsettled. She headed up the hill toward the main building of the center. Maybe her uneasy feelings were just guilt over having slept so long when she should have been working.

She unlocked the back door of the center and walked over to a white board where they kept a record of activity. All the chores, cage cleaning, feeding and medicine had been checked off. Cassidy had gone out on one call. Her note on the board said "unable to locate the hawk." A note with Jenna's name on it was pinned to the wall beside the board. Jenna pressed open the piece of paper.

Everything went really smoothly today. Your friend stayed and helped take up the slack so you could sleep. He even went out on the call with me. Nice guy. Call Peter Hickman about the upcoming fundraiser. Mrs. Ephron said there is a bear carcass on her property that is attracting a lot of scavenger birds. She wants us to come and take the birds away, like that is part of our job description. Why doesn't she just get rid of the carcass? You might want to go out there and calm her down. You know how she is.
Cassidy

Jenna smiled as she folded the note. Last spring, Mrs. Ephron had repeatedly called them because she was convinced that eagles were carrying her kittens away. But the smile faded as Jenna realized that was the second call in a week they had gotten about bear carcasses and nuisance birds. The first one had been on the property right next to Mrs. Ephron. Maybe the bears were getting into some kind of poison that was killing them. The game warden might want to look at the carcass.

She put the note in her pocket, grateful for Cassidy's recap of the day. She knew she could trust the other woman's report. Cassidy was more than a coworker. She was a good friend. After the drama with her father had happened a year ago, Cassidy was the one that picked up on her distraction despite her efforts at hiding it. Cassidy had taken her to her first Al-Anon meeting.

Jenna turned away from the white board and looked around the center. All the birds were settled behind their curtains. Cassidy was right. Keith was a nice guy. At least what she had seen of him. She had a feeling though that Keith was like an iceberg. What she saw of him was only the smallest part.

Jenna double-checked to make sure the lock on the back door was secure before entering the office area. Freddy was resting in his cage.

It was still too early in the day for him. Nighttime was his high activity time. The center's one and only desktop computer was turned off. She phoned the game warden about the bear carcasses and left a message. Then there was just one more stop to make.

She opened the front door and stepped out into the softening light of the summer evening. Her calves strained as she made her way up the hill to where the ambassador birds were housed.

She breathed a sigh of relief when she saw the padlock on the building was still in place. She filed through her keys and unlocked the door. The building was no more than an uninsulated barn divided into six sections, each stall was set up to house an education bird. In the winter, when it got below zero, the birds were often brought inside to keep them warm, but the current late-summer temperatures shouldn't be a problem for them.

The first two stalls on either side were empty. In the third stall, Jenna passed a rough-legged hawk with a wing that had been deformed at birth. She checked on the bald eagle whose beak had been shot off. An engineer at a nearby college had helped create a prosthetic beak so the animal could eat. The opposite stall contained an osprey that was blind in one eye.

An unusual amount of light seemed to be coming from the final stall where Georgina the turkey vulture resided. Jenna's heart skipped a beat as her rib cage tightened. She took the final step that allowed for a view of Georgina.

Her hand jerked to her mouth as her heartbeat sped up. At the back of the stall, someone had sawed a hole, reached in and taken Georgina.

Jenna sucked in a breath of air and shook her head trying to fight off the encroaching devastation. What good did locks do when the buildings were so flimsy?

She darted out of the barn and ran around to where the building had been cut into. Poor Georgina. Vultures were not known as the eye candy of the raptor world, but unlike so many of the birds, Georgina liked people. She walked up to volunteers and picked at their shoelaces when they brought her food in. Would she have even struggled when someone came in after her? Jenna ran her fingers along the jagged cut before studying the area around her. If a person crouched and used a hand saw, he wouldn't have been visible from the rest of the center. This barn was far enough away from the other buildings that during the day when there was a lot activity and people, the culprit wouldn't have been heard, either. She usually checked on the birds at the end of the day before locking up, but maybe the volunteers hadn't done that.

When she stood up, the rock path from her house to the main building was visible down the hill as was much of the center, but not the parking lot. It would have been easier to break into the flight barn, but it was too close to her house. Where had the thief taken Georgina? She glanced up the hill. That would be quite a hike holding a turkey vulture.

She raced down the hill, back toward her house. By the time she got to the door, she was out of breath. She fumbled with the lock and swung the door open. Jenna grabbed the phone and dialed the sheriff.

The deputy answered. Jenna explained what had happened.

The deputy said he would be right out and then asked her what a turkey vulture looked like.

"I'll find a picture." Jenna hung up, skirted to her laptop and opened up her photo file. They took pictures of all the ambassador birds for promotional purposes. She clipped through the photos until she found one of Georgina, turned on her printer and clicked the print command.

Jenna stood up and placed her hands on her hips. Despair seeped through her. Even though this was a sparsely populated county with low crime, the rest of the world probably wasn't as bent out of shape about a missing bird as she was.What else could she do? Jump in the car and search the countryside for Georgina? Put up "have you seen my bird" posters? Demand that the sheriff get search warrants for all the surrounding houses? Jenna slipped down into a chair and placed her face in her hands. Who was she kidding? That bird was gone.

Message received loud and clear. The culprits had made good on their threat. She would quit looking around on the King Ranch. She couldn't risk more harm coming to the birds in the center. She hung her head. She would just have to let it go.

"What are you doing?" Keith snapped out when he saw that after all the talk about security, she had left the door wide open.

She jumped in her chair and whirled, knocking over the stack of papers she had piled on the other chair before she shot to her feet. "What are you shouting at me for, and what are you doing barging in here?"

"Anyone could have walked in here." He gestured toward the open door. "What were you thinking?"

Jenna opened her mouth as if to speak, but instead she shook her head.

All day since he had left the center, he had thought about her, worried about her. While he baled hay for his grandfather, he wondered if she was okay. He hadn't intended for his concern to come out in anger. But when he had seen the open door, with the threats still weighing heavily on his mind, his heart had pounded against his rib cage. His first thought was that something had happened to Jenna. His second was that he should have been here to protect her.

Jenna shook her head. Disbelief clouded her features. She seemed unable to form a response. She crumpled to the floor and picked up the papers she had knocked over. She directed her comment toward the carpet, not looking up at him. "You nearly gave me a heart attack."

"I'm sorry, it's just when I saw the open door I was afraid something bad had happened to you." He turned and closed the door.

"Well, you're not wrong. Something bad did happen." She slapped a magazine back on the coffee table. "Someone cut a hole in the barn and took my turkey vulture." Agitation colored her words.

"Oh, Jenna." He rushed to her where she kneeled on the floor. "I'm sorry about the bird."

Jenna stared at the ceiling. "What am I supposed to do? This place is hardly high security. Am I supposed to get the volunteers to walk the grounds twenty-four hours a day?" Her voice broke. "Who would take a stupid turkey vulture anyway? They are the ugliest things on earth."

Jenna's eyes were glazed with tears. Keith squeezed her forearm. Her voice had trembled with fear and sadness. This was about more than the loss of the bird. She felt violated, vulnerable.

Keith swallowed hard to quell the ire he felt for whoever had done this to her. He brushed his hand over her soft hair. He waited until he could speak without showing his anger. "Please consider keeping Jet here. He's a good watchdog."

She pulled back from him, seeming unaware of his request. "This has to have happened because of that threat. I'll just do like they say and stop looking around on your grandfather's ranch. You and the sheriff can figure it out."

He doubted that would stop the vandalism. These guys were ruthless and determined to hurt her. "Jet can just stay in your house." That way at least she would be safe. Though she had not been threatened directly, the boldness of an intruder coming onto this property in broad daylight made him wonder if the level of violence might escalate. "He's a quiet guy—he's only going to bark when there is a good reason to."

She gathered more papers off the floor. "I'll be okay."

"Wouldn't it be better to have the birds a little ruffled rather than have something happen to them?"

"I appreciate the offer, but it just won't work." She slammed a magazine on top of another.

Keith tried to loosen the tightness through his chest by taking a deep breath. He couldn't just leave her here alone unprotected. "Maybe we can get the sheriff to patrol by here."

"Maybe." Lost in thought, Jenna traced her collarbone with a narrow finger. "The deputy will be here in a minute." She blew out a huff of air. "I'm sure this will provide a good laugh for them. Silly Jenna and her kidnapped bird."

"I don't think they will treat it like a joke. Too much has happened. It's got to be connected. Someone who would go to these extremes has something to hide." Anger flared anew in his muscles. The only way to end this—the threats and the fear and the trespassing on Gramps's land—was to catch the people who were doing it.

"Thanks for your vote of confidence." She

slumped in a chair. "Why were you stopping by here, anyway?"

"Craig Smith bought a bull from Gramps. I told him I would deliver it."

A faint smile lit up Jenna's heart-shaped face. "This is a little out of the way from Craig Smith's ranch."

Heat rushed to his face over her realizing he'd come here to check on her.

There was a soft rapping at the door. Keith strode across the carpet and opened it. The deputy stood at attention. His face was flushed as if he had been running. Jenna came up behind Keith.

The deputy rubbed his Adam's apple. "I found your bird." His tone indicated that it wasn't good news.

Jenna gasped. "Where?"

"On the road up here. It was…uh…hung in a tree. Whoever did it wanted the bird to be seen from the road. I don't need to see a picture. I could tell it was a vulture."

A faint moan escaped Jenna's lips.

Keith rubbed Jenna's arm. Already, her gaze indicated that she was staring at some unseen thing in the distance. He knew that look. He'd seen it in the eyes of a hundred fellow soldiers when he'd worked as a combat medic. The loss of a bird didn't compare to combat, but the emotional meltdown could be the same. He had to get her out of here, get her mind off all of this.

"Deputy, can I talk to you for a minute?"

The deputy nodded.

Keith ushered the young man outside. "You are going to look around and see if you can figure out who did this, right?"

The deputy ran his hand over his buzz cut. "Sure. I doubt I'll find anything, though. Sheriff and I went over the place pretty thoroughly last night. Probably the same guys, huh?"

Keith nodded. "The crimes these people are willing to commit just keep getting worse. I'm concerned about Jenna's safety."

"Understandable. I can stay until I get off shift or get another call. After that, the sheriff can patrol a couple of times tonight."

"That will help." Jenna was so protective of the birds at the center. For sure, she wouldn't leave them and stay at the farmhouse with his grandparents or go to a friend's house. He'd have to figure something else out.

The deputy nodded. "Guess I'll go have another look around."

Jenna came to the door and leaned against the frame. "The barn where the vulture was taken is up the hill." A veil seemed to have fallen over her eyes. She lifted her chin to show that she was doing okay, but he saw the quiver in her lips.

"Jenna, how about you and I go for a drive? The deputy can stay and keep an eye on things for a while."

The stricken look on Jenna's face concerned him. How much more would she have to take?

SEVEN

With a heavy heart, Jenna crawled up into the high seat of the old truck. Keith wasn't driving his old blue Dodge. This was a bigger truck, better suited for hauling the trailer with the bull. Jet whimpered and scooted toward the middle of the seat to make room for her.

The door on the driver's side creaked when Keith opened it and positioned himself behind the wheel. The entire truck bounced as he settled in the seat. He tried to shut the door, but it wouldn't catch. He shook it, trying to line it up with the truck's frame. "These old farm vehicles." He opened the door and slammed it again.

Keith started the truck and turned it around in the parking lot. Hindered by the weight of the trailer with the bull, the vehicle lurched forward.

Jenna was barely aware of their bumpy

progress. The shaky feeling that had invaded her limbs when she first saw the hole in Georgina's stall had subsided, but her temples still throbbed. A sense of rage over what happened made it hard for her to think.

Whoever was doing this was smart. The culprit knew that law enforcement wouldn't get overly excited about dead birds, but that it would shut her down.

As if sensing her anger, Jet licked her hand. She rubbed the dog's head and released a slow stream of air. She felt so helpless. What could she do?

The countryside had a warm glow. Flat fields abundant with crops rolled on for miles. The field changed from the green of alfalfa to golden barley: high enough for harvest and populating both sides of the road. Gossamer clouds, that looked like they had been brushstroked on the sky, blended into a soft pink at the horizon. All of it made a beautiful picture, but she was in no mood to appreciate it.

What choice did she have? If she backed off, her birds could be safer, but others, like Keith and his grandparents, could be at risk. *Something* was going on at King Ranch, and Keith and Jenna must be getting close to finding out what it was if someone would go as far as they had.

Jenna placed a hand on the dashboard when Keith drove over a bumpy part of the road. "You don't think they will leave me and the birds alone now, do you?"

Keith's shoulders stiffened and he straightened his back. "It's not a chance I would take. They might retaliate for something the sheriff finds out, whether it comes from you or not."

Jenna massaged her temples. Keith might be right about the culprits hurting her if the sheriff kept looking around. Maybe all this was revenge for alerting the sheriff in the first place. "I'm sure they took Georgina because of what we saw in the canyon. We were getting pretty close to something we weren't supposed to know about."

"But what?" Keith adjusted his hand on the steering wheel. "Hiding the fact that a bunch of guys on four-wheelers trespassed to build a fire and go joyriding wouldn't be worth that kind of effort."

Jenna clenched her teeth. This was nerveracking.

Jet whimpered.

Keith glanced at her. "You sure you don't want Jet at the center?"

"He seems really attached to you." She stroked the dog's head. "Wouldn't you miss him?"

Like a flare blazing across the night sky, Jenna detected an intense flash of emotion on Keith's face. "He's good for people." His face turned to stone again.

She longed for him to let her in. There was a big chunk of his life he was unwilling to share. "He's been good for you. That's what you meant, right?"

Keith set his jaw. "I like his company."

Warmth pooled around her heart. Keith's offer to loan her Jet had been more of a sacrifice than she had realized. "What made you decide to get a dog?"

"The military gave him to me after I was discharged." His fingers flexed nervously on the steering wheel. "You don't get out of Iraq working as a combat medic without some consequences." He offered her a furtive glance and then focused on his driving.

The hardening of his expression told her that he didn't want to tell her anything more, but she appreciated the little bit he had been willing to share.

Jenna crossed her arms and tilted her head. "It was only one eagle. Maybe I should just let it go."

Keith smiled as he turned the huge steering wheel. "I know you, Jenna. You have a strong sense of justice. There is more going on than just an eagle being shot at. You can't let it go."

"It bothers you, too."

Keith rubbed the stubble on his cheek. "Let's not think about it right now. Both of us getting worked up over it won't change a thing."

Keith let up on the accelerator. In the distance, farm outbuildings came into view. A barn leaning to one side and in need of paint rested beside a newer metal building. Farther up the hill, a trailer house and a small shed were positioned. Trucks, a car and a large combine populated the area between the buildings.

The truck swayed as they made their way up the rutty dirt road. The entire vehicle creaked and continued to shake a few seconds after Keith brought it to a stop and killed the motor. "Believe it or not, Gramps keeps the engine in this thing in tiptop shape."

Jenna nodded. "I believe you." She had been around ranchers long enough to know that the successful ones cared more about having equipment run good rather than look good. She patted the duct-taped dashboard. "It's a good truck."

Keith bent his head as a faint smile crossed his face.

A forty-something man emerged from the trailer. The fedora he wore looked out of place with the western cut shirt and cowboy boots. Craig Smith had only been running the ranch for a few years since his uncle had died, so Jenna really didn't know much about him. He had grown up in a town about fifty miles from here.

Jenna had worked with him briefly to deal with some abandoned baby owls he had found in his barn last spring. He had been helpful in transporting the owls. She'd given him a tour of the center, and he had written her a small support check. He had pulled her Subaru out of a snow bank last winter. That had been the extent of their interaction. He seemed like a nice guy, if a bit of a loner. Far as she knew, Craig had never been married and had no children.

Keith leaped out of the truck and sauntered over to Craig. He stuffed his buckskin work gloves in the back pocket of his jeans. Craig pointed to a corral by the barn, probably where he wanted the bull. The two men spoke for a minute before Keith sauntered back to the passenger side of the car and hooked his fingers on the rolled down window.

"I've just got to back up the trailer and unload him. It won't take but a minute."

Craig came up behind him. "Coffee is on inside, if you want some."

"Thanks." Jenna jumped out of the truck. Jet stayed in the cab.

Keith was already backing up the truck and trailer when she stepped into Craig's double-wide. The living space was tidy, but obviously no woman lived here. No knickknacks populated the shelves. The windows didn't have any curtains. The canisters on the counter consisted of recycled coffee cans and mismatched plastic and ceramic containers. Several decks of cards and poker chips cluttered the rest of the counter.

Jenna hadn't meant to snoop, but the "past due" stamp on two unfolded bills caught her attention. She turned away. Craig's finances were none of her business. They were probably no different than any other rancher's. For most ranchers, breaking even was considered a good year. People didn't pursue this profession to get rich. It seemed a little odd that he'd be investing in a bull if money was tight, but it was really none of her concern, so she put it out of her mind.

She retrieved a coffee cup from the dish rack, poured a cup and stirred in sugar. The coffee was smooth, no acid aftertaste.

Still holding her cup of coffee, Jenna stepped on the porch. Over by the metal building, Craig used hand signals to help Keith position the trailer holding the bull. Jet's head was visible in the cab of the truck as it slipped out of view. Keith killed the engine and jumped from the cab, disappearing behind the metal building. She heard the screeching of the metal gate on the trailer opening and the two men shouting. A moment later, a muscular black Angus bull romped to the edge of the corral.

Keith emerged from behind the building. He stopped to lean on the metal fence, obviously admiring the bull. The late-in-the-day sun gave his brown hair a golden glow. He turned toward her, smiling. Ranching work seemed to come naturally to him. She wondered how long he planned on staying around to help his grandparents.

Jenna gripped her coffee cup a little tighter. Why was she even thinking about how long he'd be staying? She would enjoy the summer with him...as a friend. Any other thought of him she needed to banish from her head.

Keith let Jet out of the truck and tossed a ball for him. Keith's laughter and cajoling along with Jet's barking floated up the hill.

Jenna took another sip of coffee and though she tried to enjoy the serenity of her surroundings, anxiety plagued her. Craig emerged from behind the metal building and strode toward the double-wide. When he was close enough for Jenna to hear, he said, "Got to get my checkbook."

"Thanks for the coffee." Jenna lifted the cup. "It was good."

"It's my specialty. I'm not much for cooking, but a good cup of coffee will wash down the worst meal."

"You have a real nice place here."

Craig wiped the sweat from his brow. "Thanks, but I inherited a lot more debt than I did land. Kind of hard to stay afloat." He grinned. "I need to win the lottery." He slipped inside the trailer and returned a moment later. He rested the open checkbook on the two-by-four railing.

Jenna looked off to the east. The outline of Angel's Wing Mountain told her which way the King Ranch was in relationship to Craig's place. If she remembered correctly, they shared a boundary. Maybe all this trouble extended beyond the King Ranch.

"Norman and Etta are having some issues with trespassers. You ever catch anyone on your land?" Even as she asked the question, fear crept back into her awareness. Just asking questions couldn't hurt. She'd pass the information on to the sheriff.

Craig shook his head. "No. Course, this place

is huge. There are remote parts of it I haven't seen."

She set her coffee cup on the railing. "I don't suppose you have noticed a helicopter flying around."

Craig closed his checkbook and put it in his breast pocket. "I've seen a couple. People use them to check cows in the high country."

True, a helicopter wasn't unheard of, though they were still pretty uncommon. "Do you know anyone who owns a helicopter?"

He studied her for a moment before shaking his head. "No, can't say as I do."

His probing gaze made Jenna uncomfortable. She ran her finger around the rim of the coffee cup. He probably wondered why she was asking so many questions.

Craig's mentioning the vastness of the ranches needled at her. A person wouldn't have to store a helicopter where it could be found. These ranches had all sorts of places a helicopter could be hidden. Her memory of the helicopter was vivid, but asking the sheriff to search landing pads and barns for it would probably be futile.

Craig rested his elbows on the railing. "Be nice if one of my neighbors did have a helicopter. I rent both a chopper and pilot out of Billings when I need one."

Keith strode up to the porch with Jet trailing behind him. He still had on his buckskin work gloves and his forehead glistened with sweat. His demeanor seemed renewed and exuberant.

Craig handed him the check. "Say hello to Norm for me."

Keith held up the check. "Gramps will appreciate you paying on time."

"Like we agreed. Half now. Half when I get the money from the grain."

Keith nodded, then turned toward Jenna. "Ready to go?"

They walked back down the hill to the truck. After helping Jet up, Jenna climbed in. Keith pushed on the gear shift, and the truck lumbered forward. The black dog panted beside her as the big truck inched along the road, shaking from side to side.

She rested against the worn seat. Her nerves felt a little more settled. "Thank you for taking me away from the center. It helped."

"No problem."

"I bet your grandparents appreciate having you around to help. Is this a long-term thing?" She couldn't help herself. She had to know.

Keith shook his head. "Just 'til the end of the summer."

So that was that. Keith had only come

for a visit. Jenna stared out at the passing landscape and tried to ignore the twinge of disappointment.

"I can come by tomorrow and get that hole boarded up for you," Keith offered.

"I'm sure you have lots to do at the ranch." His kindness touched her. "One of the volunteers can do it."

"Have you taken the keys away from the volunteers like I suggested?"

"My volunteers are all good people." Feeling defensive, her back muscles tensed. "Whoever did this didn't need a key, anyway." She did not want to believe that anyone who worked at the center would have anything to do with this.

"The person that took that bird had a working knowledge of the layout of the center."

"A lot of people come and go at the center." All the calm she had felt dissipated. "Those volunteers love the birds as much as I do." Even as she protested, she knew Keith was right. Anyone could have broken in.

She couldn't trust anyone.

Keith softened his tone. "I'm sure they are good people." His intent hadn't been to upset Jenna. He just wanted her to be safe. The whole thing enraged him. Other than the warning across his grandparents' door, he'd been left alone. What kind of a lowlife would go after a vulnerable woman living alone?

"Besides, it's the birds that are being targeted...not me."

"I hope that remains the case." He didn't want to make her afraid, but she needed to be realistic about the danger.

When he pulled into the center's parking lot, the deputy's car was gone.

Jenna's hand touched her cheek as she voiced the same thought that ran through his head. "The deputy must have gotten called out for something."

"The sheriff is going to patrol by here a couple times." Frustration coiled inside him. A few drive-bys wouldn't be enough to assure him that she would be okay. "I just wish you had a better security system."

"We're doing our big fundraiser ball at Peter Hickman's in two days." She pushed open the door and hopped down. "Purchasing some sort of alarm system just moved to the top of my wish list."

"Make sure you lock your door and don't go out until Cassidy gets here in the morning."

"Keith, I'm not twelve years old. I have to check on the birds in the night." She raised an eyebrow as if to challenge any objection he might give her. "See ya." She closed the door of the truck.

Jenna waved as she walked past the windshield. Keith watched as she checked the front door on the center to make sure it was locked before heading to the stone path.

Uneasiness spread through Keith as he watched Jenna heading down the hill to her house. Would she be okay tonight?

Jenna's long hair waved in the breeze like a delicate silk scarf. He waited until she unlocked the door and was safely inside before he pulled out of the lot and drove back home.

Etta King was standing in the front yard when he pulled up to the farmhouse. She yanked off her garden gloves after setting a trowel on a stump by the door. "Got some lasagna in the oven if you're hungry, Keith."

"That sounds good, Grandma." Despite years of hard work and harsh winters, Etta King projected a youthful energy with her rosy cheeks and perfect posture. Her long silver-white hair was twisted up on top of her head.

He glanced at their front door. He and Jenna had scrubbed so thoroughly that no trace of the warning written in blood remained. He had told them about the trespassers; they needed to know that much.

"You been out helping that Jenna Murphy today?" Etta's blue eyes had a vibrant sparkle to them.

Keith hesitated. He didn't want to alarm his grandparents, but they needed to be aware of what was going on. "Yes, she had some trouble over at the rescue center. There was a break-in and today someone killed one of the birds."

Etta covered her mouth with one hand and shook her head. "That poor girl. I'll keep her in my prayers." Etta stared off in the distance. "Who would do such a thing? Used to be, you knew who your neighbors were around here."

Her voice trailed off and he knew she was thinking about the trespassers as well as what had happened to Jenna. He rested a hand on her thin shoulder. "I am going to get to the bottom of this, Grandma."

She managed a smile. "I know you will." They walked into the kitchen together.

Italian spices swirled in the humidity from the oven's heat. His mouth watered. No one could make lasagna like Grandma.

"I always did like Jenna. Don't seem to run into her much anymore. She was such a sweetheart when she was a teenager."

Remorse spread through him. "Not like me, huh?"

Etta faced her grandson. "What is past is past, Keith." She cupped a hand on each of his shoulders. She was so short that she had to stand on tiptoe. "You are not that troubled boy anymore, and we are glad to have you here."

He couldn't undo the past; he could only make amends. Sometimes though, the guilt ate at him.

Norman King appeared in the doorway. "What cha got cookin' in there, Mother? Smells like an Italian diner."

Etta bustled over to the oven. "Got some garlic bread and salad made with lettuce from the garden and homemade vinaigrette to go with the lasagna."

Norman rubbed his gnarled hands together. He wiggled his bushy eyebrows at Keith. "Sounds good, doesn't it, son?"

Keith smiled. He was twenty-nine. He'd faced death and worse. And his grandparents still talked to him like he was a kid. There was something endearing about that.

His grandfather shuffled over to the table. Keith pulled Craig's check for the bull out of his back pocket and handed it to Norman. The old man moved a lot slower than he had twelve years ago. The years had passed too quickly. Keith had been too wounded to accept the love they offered all those years ago. He was happy to accept it now, but chances were his future job would take him out of state. He only hoped to be able to visit them for many more years.

Etta set the steaming casserole dish on the table. "Keith's been helping Jenna Murphy over at the bird place she runs."

Norman plumped down in a chair and stuffed a fabric napkin into his collar. "I always did like that girl."

"She goes to that church over on Beacon Street now, but I see her once a year when all the churches get together for the annual garage sale. Such a sweetie." She held out her hand to Keith. "Hand me your plate, dear."

Keith shifted in his chair. If he didn't know better, he'd say that his grandparents were matchmaking. "I'm just here until the end of summer."

Etta piled the lasagna on Keith's plate and then sat down, lacing her fingers together. "I'm only saying how nice she is."

They bowed their heads and said grace.

Norman scooted his chair closer to the table. "Been thinking about fixing up some fence in the northern quarter."

"I can give you a hand with that." Keith grabbed a piece of garlic bread. He had vowed to make sure that anytime his grandfather went to the remote parts of the ranch, he would go, too. He didn't want to think about what would happen if his grandfather stumbled on the trespassers.

They discussed the repairs that needed to be done on the tractor before harvest time and other things. After dinner, Keith spent some time watching television with them before heading up to his place.

He fell into his bed and slept for a few hours. When he awoke, it was still dark outside. He had yet to sleep a full eight hours since his discharge. He lifted the thin blanket and sauntered over to his easel. A canyon with a silver and blue river roaring through it was starting to come to life on the canvas. He and Jenna had rafted this river together.

He squeezed out some white on his palette. They had just been kids having fun back then. Rock climbing and rafting were a lot different than a relationship. As easy as it was to be with her, it didn't make sense to start anything now.

He was still alert after painting for several hours. He opened his Bible and read for a while. Jenna's weary, anxious look from earlier kept flashing through his mind. That uneasy feeling that snaked around his rib cage returned. He wasn't going to sleep anymore tonight.

"Come on, Jet. Let's go make ourselves useful."

He padded softly down the stairs. The lights were out in his grandparents' place so he was as quiet as possible as he started up the old Dodge. The headlights cut a swath of illumination as he rumbled down the road. He was sure everything was fine—Jenna was right when she said the birds had been targeted, not her—but he knew he wouldn't feel easy again until he saw that she was safe with his own two eyes.

He pulled into the dark parking lot and retrieved his cell phone. He'd probably be waking her, but that would be better than scaring her by making her think he was an intruder. He was surprised when she picked up after the first ring.

"Hello." She didn't sound like she had been sleeping.

"Jenna, it's me, Keith."

"I know, I saw the caller ID." A second of silence filled the line. "Besides, I know your voice."

"I'm in the center parking lot." When he leaned his head sideways, he saw that her living room lights were on. "I thought I would watch the place for a couple of hours."

Jenna sighed audibly. "Thank you. I haven't been able to sleep a wink. Every noise makes me jump. But what are you doing up?"

Thinking about you.

"I keep kind of strange hours." He scooted across the seat. She was visible in the living room window. "It's a holdover from Iraq. I sleep lightly and in short intervals."

She turned facing the window so she was looking directly at his truck. "That sounds like a lot to deal with."

"Sometimes it is." The compassion he heard in her voice made him want to share more, but maybe this wasn't the time. He shifted on the seat so he could see her better. She waved from the window. Light washed over her, making her hair appear glittery and her expression bright.

After saying goodbye, Keith hung up and grabbed a flashlight from his glove compartment. He walked the grounds with Jet padding silently behind him. The stillness of the night surrounded him. He patrolled for several minutes and then returned to the truck. Unless someone hiked in from the hills, the only access to the center was on the road behind him. He'd be able to see headlights way before they got to the center. He rolled down the window to catch any out-of-place noises.

Jenna's living room light clicked off.

Maybe now at least one of them would get some sleep.

EIGHT

Though Jenna could not discern words, Cassidy's voice sounded frantic. Distortion on the line made it hard for Jenna to understand her assistant.

Pressing the phone harder against her ear, Jenna paced through the raptor center. "What did you say?"

"I said I'm pretty sure I just saw a bird, an eagle, shot out of the sky."

Ice froze in Jenna's veins. "Where...where are you?" She sank into a chair as the numbness invaded her limbs.

"Gleason's Road just west of the center, but the bird was off in the distance." Static broke up her words. "It will take a while to figure out where it went down."

"I'll come out and help you. Do you mind waiting?"

"I can start looking."

"No." Jenna's heart squeezed tight. "Don't start searching for it alone." She didn't want to alarm her friend but given what had happened the last few days, if the shooter was still around, Cassidy might be in danger. "Stay close to your car and just wait for me, okay?"

"Okay," Cassidy said. "You think this has something to do with the vandalism?"

"We can't take that chance." Cassidy knew most of the details of everything that had happened.

Jenna grabbed her purse and headed out to her Subaru. Keith stood in the parking lot holding a cardboard box. For a guy who never slept, he looked pretty good. The teal shirt he wore gave his eyes a bluish hue. The five o'clock shadow and ruffled hair made him look rugged but not unkempt.

"Back already?"

When she had awakened this morning, his truck was gone. His coming to keep vigil over the center was just what she had needed to finally get some sleep.

He lifted the box toward her. "I was in town and I found this motion sensitive light at the pawnshop. It's not a whole security system, but it will help. I can install it."

His thoughtfulness warmed her heart, but

panic over what might have happened to the eagle and concern for Cassidy overtook her good feelings. She ran her fingers through her long hair. "Thank you. You can just leave it inside with one of the volunteers."

"What's wrong?" Keith stepped closer, his eyes searching. "You seem upset."

She never could hide her emotions from him. "Cassidy thinks she saw an eagle being shot. I'm going out to see if we can find where the bird went down."

"I'll go with you." He placed the box beside the door and turned to face her.

"We'll take my car." She had no desire to argue with him about joining her. She had no idea what she and Cassidy might be facing. Having Keith along sounded like a good idea.

Keith opened the passenger-side door and pulled out the dry-cleaning bag she had hung over the seat.

"That's my dress for the fundraiser tomorrow night. Just toss it in the back."

Jenna drove a little too fast over the gravel road. Her heart raced as she fought to keep panicked thoughts at bay. If this bird had been shot, it meant the eagles were being targeted. The first eagle hadn't just been an isolated incident.

Jenna sailed over a bump and the car caught

air. The impulse to get there and get there fast made it hard for her to slow down.

Keith cleared his throat, but didn't say anything. She noticed he gripped the handle of the door.

She took in a cleansing breath and let up on the accelerator.

Jenna rounded a hill. Cassidy's white truck was visible in the early evening light. She must have been looking for Jenna in the rearview mirror because she had opened the door and stepped out by the time Jenna brought the car to a stop.

Cassidy walked over to them while they got out of the car. Her blond hair was pulled back from a face etched with worry.

Jenna stood beside her friend. "Where did you see the bird?"

A flat area with clumps of grass stretched out from the road and went on for a mile or so. Forest to the east and west and buttes to the south bordered the flat area.

The sky took up three quarters of the view. "I was driving home when I spotted the eagle soaring." Cassidy pointed up midway in the sky. "I stopped the car to get out and watch him. They are so beautiful when they fly, so carefree."

The sight of a soaring raptor had always filled Jenna's heart with admiration, too.

"And then," Cassidy continued as she drew the path of the bird across the sky, "I heard a sound. I can't say for sure that it was a gunshot. But…he wobbled and spiraled downward."

"Do you think he landed in the flat area?" Keith paced away from the road, studying the area around him.

Cassidy nodded. "I got out my binoculars and started looking." She touched her fingers to her lips. "I couldn't see any kind of movement on the ground." Sorrow permeated her voice.

It was a lot of territory to cover, but the probability of finding the bird was far greater than if he had gone down in the trees. "The three of us can do a grid search."

Jenna's gaze scanned the open area. If someone had shot a bird, where would they have hidden? The trees provided cover. If they lay on their stomach, the rolling hills that jutted up against the buttes would be a good place to hide. She shivered. Was the shooter still out there?

It didn't make sense to call the sheriff unless they found something. She had been seeing way more of Sheriff Douglas in the last few days than she did all year. If the eagle had been shot, it was a crime, and they would have to report it, but first they needed to find the eagle.

"I can only give a rough estimate of where I think I saw it go down." Cassidy's shoulders jerked. "I was looking away when it registered in my brain what might have happened."

"So maybe he was just diving?" Anxiety made Jenna's stomach churn. She did not want to find a dead eagle.

"Maybe." Cassidy didn't sound too hopeful. "He was moving across the sky and then he was gone."

Jenna ran to her car and grabbed two pairs of binoculars. She handed one to Keith. He must have picked up on her fear because he leaned close and whispered, "It's gonna be okay."

The small assurance bolstered her resolve. "How far out do you think we need to walk?"

Cassidy retrieved her binoculars from the bumper of her truck. "It was closer to the buttes than the road. I'd say we need to hike almost all the way out there."

"Okay, let's spread out."

Cassidy placed her hands on her hips. "About thirty yards apart should do it. If we can't find him, we can't find him."

Of course, Jenna knew Cassidy wouldn't give up as easily as her words implied. Neither would she. They would stay out here until dark if they had to.

Jenna paced out toward the buttes, examining the ground in front of her and to each side. She ran a little faster, still scanning the hard earth for the distinctive white feathers, knowing that the eagle could be hidden by the tufts of grass and rock.

Once she reached the base of the rolling hills, she jogged out ten yards toward the trees and then turned and faced the road and parked cars. When she looked up, Cassidy's blond hair was easy enough to spot. Jenna worked her way closer to the road and then whirled around to do another trek back to the buttes.

More determined than ever, she continued to search. Some of the tension in her muscles subsided when she saw Keith working his way east. The light had begun to dim, making it harder to see him.

Jenna headed back toward the buttes again. Her feet pounded out a rhythm. She stopped to study the ground. The eagle's coloring was designed to help him blend into his surroundings. Years of bird spotting, though, had trained her eyes to separate wild animal from wilderness.

She stepped forward. Her heart stopped. Ten yards in front of her was a lump that didn't look like grass. She took two big strides and then ran. Instantly, she dropped to her knees. Sorrow flooded through her as wind rustled the feathers of the dead bird. She reached out a hand to touch its head. The mature bald eagle had had at least a six-foot wing span. It must have been beautiful in flight.

Her hand trailed down to the bloody breast feathers.

She heard pounding footsteps and then Keith knelt beside her. He gasped in air from running.

She touched the bloody spot. "That is a bullet hole, isn't it?"

His voice was gentle. "Yes. It's a clean shot." He turned, looking at the area that surrounded them. "If Cassidy never saw the shooter, he must have had a high-powered rifle with a good sight on it."

"We have proof now that someone's doing this on purpose. The sheriff doesn't seem to be able to make much progress. This is clearly poaching. We can bring the game warden in on this." Jenna clenched her teeth, trying to hold back the rising tide of fury.

"Somebody is sure gutsy." Keith rose to his feet. "Do you know who owns this land?"

"It's government land." Jenna rocked back and forth. She couldn't get a deep breath because of the tightness in her chest. "I don't know who is leasing it. Mrs. Ephron's acre of land isn't far from here."

"Gramps's place is behind us." He pivoted. "It's all happening in the same area."

Jenna heard Cassidy's hurried footsteps.

Cassidy dropped down beside her friend. Her breath caught. A faint moan escaped her lips.

"I'll have to wait here until the game warden comes," Jenna said. "No doubt this bird was a trophy to someone and they might come back for it. She had a feeling Cassidy had interrupted the hunt. The tail feathers and the talons all had monetary value—maybe that was why they were being hunted.

"I can wait with you," Cassidy offered.

"You go on home. I'll stay here with her," Keith said.

As she stared at the dead bird, its feathers ruffled by the breeze, Keith's voice sounded so far away.

Cassidy wrapped her arm around Jenna and squeezed her shoulder. She could barely feel Cassidy's touch. It was as if she were experiencing everything underwater.

"I'll call the warden before I leave," Cassidy said.

Jenna uttered a "thank you" though her voice did not sound like her own.

* * *

Keith leaned close to Jenna. He touched her face at the jawline and gently turned her head away from the bird. "Don't torture yourself by looking." The devastation on her face floored him.

"I'm going to get to the bottom of this." Anger colored her words. "I'll do everything I can to make sure the warden finds this guy."

He could only hope that the warden and not Jenna found the shooter first. The resolve he heard in her voice told him nothing would deter her. He couldn't blame her for her anger. But the thought of Jenna confronting someone brutal and arrogant with no respect for life made Keith's heart clench in fear.

Jenna sat back on the ground. Keith scooted up toward her. On the road, Cassidy waved at them before getting into her truck.

Jenna dug her heels into the earth. "This bird was killed with a bullet from a rifle, not a shot-gun. Bullets can be traced."

Keith's gaze darted from one high place on the landscape to another. They were exposed if they stayed out here. "Why don't we wait over by the car?"

"We can't move the bird. It's just like a regular crime scene."

Keith rose to his feet, spotted a stick a few feet away and walked over to it. "We can mark the spot and watch from the road." He pushed the stick in the ground next to the dead eagle. "Hand me your scarf."

Jenna untied the scarf from around her neck. It fluttered in the breeze as she handed it to him. Keith knotted it firmly to the stick to enable them to sight it from the road.

They walked back to the car and settled on the bumper. Jenna crossed her arms and kicked at the dirt. The wind caught her long hair and it brushed over his cheek. He'd do anything to take her anguish away. "This game warden is pretty good?"

"I don't know. He's new. I don't think we have even had a poaching case since he got the job." Frustration undergirded her words.

Keith pushed off the bumper and stalked forward a few steps. "Maybe you should let the warden do his job." The harder Jenna pushed, the more he feared for her safety.

"I will, but I am not going to stop trying to figure out who is behind this." She shifted slightly on the bumper. "I just hope I can keep the birds at the center safe. Peter's fundraiser should give us enough to buy a security system. That will help a lot."

"Who is this Peter guy, anyway? You keep talking about him." Jenna spoke so warmly of him; Keith's curiosity was piqued.

Jenna drew back as though she had been caught off guard. "He's the center's biggest supporter. Last year his fundraiser allowed us to build the flight barn. You should come to the ball. It's a lot of fun."

A fundraiser that could finance a whole security system made his motion sensitive light look like nothing. Keith rubbed the back of his neck where it had grown tense. "It's a formal thing, huh?" The thought of wearing a tie made him itch.

"The women like to go all-out, but dressed up for a Montana guy means you wear clean jeans and you scrape the mud off your boots."

The sparkle had returned to Jenna's round brown eyes and her dimple showed when she smiled. Talking about the birds did that for her.

"You are welcome to come to the event," she said.

Formal events really weren't his thing, but he didn't want to hurt her feelings.

Up the road, a dust cloud indicated that the game warden was on his way. The warden pulled over to the side of the road and opened the door. He was a weathered-looking man with white hair and a silver white beard. Though he had a start on a pot belly, his stride indicated strength.

"Keith, this is Leland Furness. Leland, this is Keith Roland, Norman King's grandson."

Leland offered Keith a handshake with a solid grip.

"Been seeing a lot of you in the last couple of days, Jenna." Leland pulled a toothpick out of his shirt pocket and rolled it around in his mouth.

"Did you check on the bear carcass on Mrs. Ephron's land?"

"Yep." Leland crossed his arms over his chest. "Carcass was pretty well consumed, hard to say what killed it. Took what samples we could."

Jenna filled the warden in on the details about the eagle and pointed to the area Keith had marked. "Do you need us to stay and help out?"

Leland shook his head. "It's a one person job. 'Bout suppertime. I'm sure you two are getting hungry."

They talked for a while longer. As Leland filled them in on what he would do, Jenna's confidence seemed to return.

Jenna thanked Leland before she and Keith got in her car and headed back to the center.

When they pulled into the center, Jenna seemed to sense his reluctance to leave her by herself. She turned to him and said, "Thank you for coming over and doing patrol last night. I see the need for extra security now. I think I am going to ask one of the volunteers to stay with me tonight. She's older and single and loves the birds as much as I do. We'll take turns checking on the birds."

He liked that she was taking steps to stay safer, but Jenna and an older lady wouldn't be much of a match for an intruder. "Can't Cassidy stay with you?"

"She's married, Keith. I am sure she wants to be with her husband."

"I still might swing by if I can't sleep."

"It should be okay. No one bothered the center last night. They must think I backed off." She took in a ragged breath. "Maybe that is why they felt so free to get back to shooting at eagles."

If the culprits found out she had called the game warden, they might come back and do more damage, she mused.

Jenna slammed her head against the back of the seat and stared at the ceiling. "What can I do? It's obvious now that the eagles are being targeted."

It bothered him that the bad guys seemed to have the upper hand. "Cassidy didn't say anything about seeing a helicopter. I wonder how that fits in."

Jenna shook her head. "When we saw the helicopter, it was midday. The trespassers and this shooting happened in the evening and late at night." After reaching back to grab her dress in the dry-cleaning bag, Jenna opened her door.

Keith got out as well and sauntered over to his truck.

She picked up the box containing the motion sensitive light. "Thanks, this was really thoughtful."

Keith said good-night and jumped into the cab of his truck. He rumbled down the road back to the ranch. The game warden had seemed hopeful about matching the bullet to a gun just like Jenna had said. But that would mean they would have to have at least one suspect and a reason to search his home for a rifle. So far, the culprits had remained invisible. The warden had said, too, that he could search the area for spent shells to find where the shooter had been. Maybe what he would be able to piece together would put an end to this. Keith wanted to believe that, still wasn't sure.

The whole time they were waiting for the game warden, Keith had that strange sensation that they were being watched. Maybe whoever had shot the bird was waiting for the chance to get his trophy. Once the game warden showed up and took the eagle, that chance had been thwarted. Certainly, that wouldn't sit easy with the shooter. But what would he do to retaliate?

Would he escalate to hurting people…like Jenna?

NINE

Keith raised the ax above his head and brought it down on the piece of wood. As he stared at the pile of wood he had chopped, a sense of satisfaction filled him. His grandparents would be cozy warm in the winter thanks to his efforts. He had had a productive day helping his grandfather. Though his arms ached some, he could feel strength returning. All in all, a good day. Or rather, it would have been if he could've stopped himself from worrying about Jenna. He knew he was overreacting. Certainly, she would have called if something had gone wrong.

Etta came and stood in the door. He knew that look on her face. The crevice between the eyebrows indicated she was anxious about something.

Keith straightened and wiped the sweat from his brow. "What is it, Grandma?"

"Didn't you say you talked to the game warden yesterday?"

Keith nodded.

Etta touched her fingers to her face. "There was a story just on the news. He was in some kind of crazy car accident. The poor man will be laid up in the hospital for weeks."

The ax felt weighted in Keith's hand as a rising sense of panic filled him. He doubted the car wreck had been an accident. Someone wanted to put the warden out of commission for a while. He pulled his cell phone off his belt and dialed Jenna's number.

His grandmother stepped toward him. "Who are you trying to call, dear?"

"Jenna…I'm just…worried about her." He squeezed the phone a little tighter. "But she is not answering."

"She's probably up at that big shindig at Peter Hickman's house. Norm doesn't feel up to going, so we are staying home. Half the town is going to be there, though."

Half the town. That meant that someone who wanted to put Jenna out of commission might be there, too.

The satin skirt of Jenna's gown rustled as she took a sip of her punch. For the third time, she looked toward the door of Peter Hickman's house, thinking she would see Keith. Apparently he had decided not to come to the fundraiser.

Cassidy bustled up to Jenna holding a small plate piled with hors d'oeuvres. She pointed to a cracker with a dollop of white stuff and green onions on it. "These are really good."

Jenna took the cracker and nibbled. The smoothness of the cream cheese mingled with spices, making her mouth water.

Cassidy tugged at the waistline of her dress. "Good turn out, huh?"

"Yes, most of the town is here." Many of the volunteers had come, but she also saw a lot of people she didn't recognize. They must be friends of Peter's. Craig Smith stood in a corner leaning close to another man in a cowboy hat.

Again, Jenna caught herself glancing at the door. The fundraiser was fun. Why then did it feel incomplete without Keith?

Cassidy leaned toward her. "I haven't seen Peter yet, have you?" She adjusted a clip in her blond hair.

Jenna shook her head. Peter's house was huge and partygoers were spread throughout it. The room they were in was open with large wooden floor-to-ceiling beams and a slate floor. A bubbling fountain served as the centerpiece. The room stretched out into a balcony where more people gathered.

A man with brassy red hair peered at them through the doorway that led to a ballroom where country music and party chatter spilled out.

"Oops, there is my hubby, better go." Cassidy placed the plate of food in Jenna's hand. "Are your feet glued to the floor?"

"No." Jenna took another bite of cracker. She set the plate on a little table. She needed to stop nervous nibbling.

"Enjoy yourself, mingle, remind people that we need donations year-round." Cassidy scooted away, hooking her arm in her husband's and disappearing into the ballroom.

Craig Smith raised his voice; his face scrunched up into a grimace as he left the man he had been talking to. He stalked past Jenna.

"How is that new bull working out?" she asked.

He stared at Jenna for a moment as though he were trying to place her. "Fine," Craig barked and headed into the ballroom.

Jenna sauntered toward the balcony where several couples had their heads bent close together. She set her drink on the railing. A cool evening breeze wafted up to her. Peter had built his house in a high spot so most of the valley was visible. Close by, she could see Peter's barn and corral that held two horses. Beyond that were the mountain peaks of the King Ranch. The water tower on Craig Smith's place was visible, as well. But despite the lovely view, she still had the urge to turn back around and see if Keith had arrived.

She leaned on the railing and closed her eyes. She really had to let go of the idea of more than a friendship with Keith. His friendship was wonderful—more than enough for her. She had been so touched by his coming to watch over the center in the middle of the night and getting her the motion sensitive light. It was just nice to know that you were in someone's thoughts.

"Just the woman I want to see."

Jenna turned to face Peter Hickman. He was a short, broad-shouldered man with a thinning hairline. Despite his lack of stature, his physique indicated that he did a great deal of physical activity. He had moved to Hope Creek for the camping, climbing and hunting opportunities, hobbies that he had made into a business. Peter owned a corporation that made heavy-duty gear for all kinds of outdoor activities from hiking to camping.

"Peter, I was wondering where you were."

"Sorry, I had some unexpected business calls." He touched his thinning hair at the temple.

"Looks like most of the town showed up this year. The turnout is even bigger than last year," Jenna said.

"You'll be glad to know we have added up the donations. I think you will be pleased with the total. I'm sure more will trickle in—some people's consciences don't get pricked until after the party. We'll make the announcement in the ballroom in a few minutes."

"I'll be ready to receive the check." Jenna took a sip of her punch. "I'm hoping to get a security system."

"Oh?" Peter leaned closer. "I thought you said something about a new X-ray machine and medical supplies."

"Priorities changed." Even talking about this made her stomach tighten. As a major sponsor of the center, Peter had the right to know the full story of what was going on, but she couldn't quite bring herself to talk about it. Not tonight. "We have had some…vandalism issues."

Jenna turned back toward the railing, and Peter sidled up beside her so they were both looking out on the property.

"That's too bad. I hope the birds weren't harmed."

"We lost one of our education birds." She struggled to keep the sadness out of her voice. "Georgina."

"The turkey vulture?"

She was delighted to hear he remembered. She had given him the tour of the place over a year ago. "Yes."

"Georgina had her charm, didn't she?"

Jenna lifted her head and laughed. "There are few people who would say that about a turkey vulture."

"And you are one of them, Jenna." Peter's voice warmed. "The work you do with these birds is important." He checked his watch. "It's about time." He held up his arm for her to take. "Shall we?"

Jenna turned. Her breath caught. Keith stood in front of her.

Keith tugged nervously at the collar of his stark white button down shirt. He had shaved and trimmed his hair. He patted his very clean jeans. "Dressed up for Montana, right?" Not that he felt dressed up, compared to the guy Jenna was with, who was wearing a suit and tie.

"You look nice," Jenna said after clearing her throat. She seemed startled to see him. Had she given up on him coming?

"You must be Peter Hickman. I'm Keith Roland, a friend of Jenna's." Keith held out his right hand on purpose so Peter would have to let go of Jenna's arm.

When he had seen Peter and Jenna together on the balcony standing near each other, he'd felt a spark of envy. They were leaning close together, and Jenna had laughed at something Peter said.

Jenna's affection for Peter must be because he cared about the birds. Peter had to be pushing fifty. All the same, Keith found himself wanting to be the one next to her, engulfed in her laughter and the sweet scent of perfume.

Jenna whirled back toward the railing and grabbed a plastic cup filled with punch, which she gulped.

"Why don't I give you and your friend a minute?" Peter suggested. "You'll hear me make the announcement over the PA. I'll talk for a while before you have to come up to accept the check and do your talk." Peter excused himself, leaving Jenna and Keith alone.

Jenna gripped her empty plastic cup. "You made it."

Her cheeks were flushed. She'd piled her hair on top of her head, revealing her long neck.

The rich burgundy color of her dress made her tanned skin appear smooth and warm.

His fingers skimmed her bare arm. "You look nice." He pulled the plastic cup, which she had nearly crushed, from her other hand. His gaze went from her full, round eyes to her lips.

"What made you decide to come?"

It would be better to tell her about the game warden later. This was her special night. "How could I not come? Everybody in town is here." He just wanted her to be safe tonight.

Peter's voice, amplified by a microphone, filled the whole house. People migrated from the balcony toward Peter.

"We should go into the ballroom," Jenna said.

He followed behind Jenna, scanning the room which was full of people. Crowds provided ample opportunity to do harm and remain anonymous. Keeping an ear tuned to the people around him, he stayed close to Jenna.

"I need to go up there." Jenna pushed her way through the crowd and stood to the side while Peter continued to talk. A cage covered in a cloth rested on a table beside Jenna. She slipped a heavy glove from the table onto her hand. While Peter talked, Jenna opened the cage door and coaxed a smaller breed hawk onto her gloved hand.

Peter announced the amount of money the event had raised for the center and the crowd clapped. He introduced Jenna as the director of the center. She stood beside Peter while they bantered about the bird she had brought with her and the work the center did. Jenna's body language toward Peter was friendly, but nothing more.

Still, the sudden surge of jealousy had surprised him.

Jenna finished her talk, the audience applauded and Peter encouraged people to enjoy themselves. Peter and Jenna pressed their heads close together and spoke for a moment.

"Hello, my friend." A cold hand cupped Keith's shoulder.

"Craig. How are things with you?"

"Good. Your grandfather raises fine Angus bulls. At least that part of ranchin' is working out."

Though Craig tried to keep the tone of the conversation friendly, his voice held an undertone of agitation and he kept glancing around the room.

Keith made small talk a while longer and then disengaged himself from the conversation. He looked at the front of the room where he thought he'd find Jenna, but he couldn't spot her.

He glanced around the room. Craig had melted into the crowd. He studied each face, not recognizing anyone.

Keith pushed through the crowd toward where Jenna had been. The cage with the bird had been taken. There must be a back door she slipped out of. Mentally, he berated himself for not keeping an eye on her. She didn't know about the warden. She didn't know she wasn't safe.

Jenna placed the bird in the back of the Subaru and closed the hatch. Her stomach was still somersaulting. Speaking in public did that to her. She didn't want to go back and face the crowd until she calmed down. Instead, she walked down the path to Peter's barn and corral. Horses didn't interest her as much as birds, but she knew Peter was proud of his new stable and she had promised to see it before she left. Now was as good a time as any.

From the time Keith had stepped in the room, she had felt like she had been caught up in a whirlwind. She'd been lying to herself. She couldn't just be friends with him.

He had changed. While she was giving her talk she had seen a waiter offer Keith a drink from a tray twice, and he had refused each time. She didn't have to be afraid of that any-more. Still, she felt a hesitation she didn't under-stand. Where was his faith at? He never talked about God.

Jenna leaned against the metal corral. One of the horses trotted toward her and nuzzled her hand. She touched his velvet nose.

Peter had said he had more horses in the barn. She opened the small door and closed it behind her. She breathed in the heady aroma of hay and manure. The room was nearly dark. She fumbled on the wall for a light switch beside the door. When she couldn't find it, she ran her hand over the wall. The aged wood of the barn prickled her fingertips.

Jenna squinted. She couldn't see much beyond shadows. From the outside, the barn appeared huge. Though the sound came from very far away, a horse stomped and snorted.

The loft above her creaked. She heard a thud that sounded like a footstep. She swept along the wall searching for a switch.

Something tickled her face. A spider, maybe? She shuddered and brushed at her cheek. When she tilted her head, a string hanging from an incandescent light bulb came into view. No light switch required. She pulled on the string.

The tiny bulb illuminated only a small area, the low end of the barn where Peter kept bags of feed. She could make out the ascending roof-line. It looked like the middle of the barn functioned as some sort of indoor arena. The horses must be on the other side of the barn in the darkness.

Jenna crossed her arms over her chest. Grappling through the dark, looking for a light switch, was not her idea of a good time. She didn't want to see the horses that badly. Her stomach had settled. Might as well get back to the party.

She pivoted to leave. The sound of wood scraping against wood reached her ears. A repetitive thundering beat dominated the space before she had taken her first step. When she turned, she was looking up the nostrils of a horse that had to be at least eighteen hands high. The horse stomped its front hoof and snorted. Someone really wasn't in the mood for visitors.

Jenna walked backward toward the door. Adrenaline kicked in; her heart pounded against her ribs. The horse continued to paw the ground with its hoof. She swiveled around to open the door and slammed against a hard muscular chest.

A strong arm grabbed her around the waist

and pulled her through the door. Still holding her, Keith leaned forward and yanked the door shut.

"You all right?"

She nodded. Keith could feel her rib cage contracting and expanding as she tried to get her breath.

Her hand rested on his bicep. "That horse gave me a scare."

He gazed down at her. "What were you doing in there?" She hadn't broken free of his grasp. He liked the way she felt in his arms.

"I…was…just going for a walk. I needed to calm my nerves. Peter mentioned he had some beautiful horses in his barn." Her lips parted. Did she want him to kiss her? The softening of her expression stirred up old feelings.

She locked into his gaze. He leaned toward her.

She eased free of his arms. Her hand brushed over his scarred wrist. "Why did you come out here?"

Keith stepped back. He had probably read the signals wrong. She hadn't wanted to kiss him. "I was worried about you. You haven't seen the news?"

She shook her head. "I've been getting ready for the fundraiser all day."

"The game warden was in a car accident. I don't know all the details, but he is going to be in the hospital for a while."

Her jaw dropped. "Which means he won't be able to look into the shooting."

"Too coincidental, don't you think?"

"But it is possible that it is a coincidence." She sounded like she was trying to convince herself.

He reached a hand toward her. "You really need to be careful. Don't take matters into your own hands."

With each word, she seemed to be retreating emotionally. Maybe it was just the leftover adrenaline from her encounter with the horse or the news about the car accident, but she seemed agitated. And her irritation was directed toward him.

"I have to do my job. I don't enjoy feeling like my hands are tied."

"I understand, but we can't ignore what has happened to the warden."

"I should get back to the house." She stalked away from him, her long dress rustling as she made her way.

Keith touched his wrist where her fingers had trailed so lightly, feeling the rough texture of the scars beneath the cotton. Seeing her look so beautiful had put him off balance. He'd been swept up in the moment. Of course, she didn't want to kiss him. And he had no interest in being hurt by her again.

TEN

Jenna eased her Subaru up the mountain road. An owl in a carrier rested in the back. A knot had formed at the base of her neck, and it wasn't just because of the hazardous driving. She was on the King Ranch again, this time with permission. She'd phoned Norman and Etta's home number and was grateful when Etta answered. Hearing Keith's voice would have been too much for her heart. They hadn't spoken since they'd gone their separate ways at the fundraiser the previous night.

Gripping the wheel, she stretched her neck side to side in an effort to release the tension.

The best survival strategy for the birds was to release them as close to where they had been found. The owl had been found in the spring on the King Ranch, so that was where she was going, even though the driving conditions were less than ideal. This road was always rutty and could be called a road only if the term was applied loosely. Rain from earlier in the day had added extra slickness.

What had happened to the game warden weighed heavily on her. But Cassidy had called in sick. Jenna had no choice but to go to the King Ranch alone. All of this was so frustrating. She needed to do her job. These people didn't have a camera in the sky. They couldn't tell where she was all the time. Still, it would have been nice to feel comfortable asking Keith to come along.

She brought the car to a stop and pushed her door open. Her feet were clumped with mud by the time she opened the hatchback. She relished the stillness of early evening and drank in the clean air. Since this bird was an owl, the best time for his release was close to dark.

Jenna pulled the carrier toward the edge of the car. She'd have to hike in to get the bird to a good release area. She knew that there was a meadow up ahead surrounded by pine trees, good owl habitat.

She grabbed her vest from the backseat, slipped into it and picked up the carrier. Releasing the birds was her favorite part of working at the center. It meant she had done her job right, one more of God's creation would thrive.

Work was a lot easier to think about than Keith. He had almost kissed her last night… and she had wanted to feel his lips against hers. A flash of fear had caused her to step back. Both of them were keeping secrets. How could a relationship move forward if he wouldn't share his past with her? And every time she thought about telling Keith about her father, shame dominated her emotions. She felt foolish for having kept the secret so long.

She hiked toward a stand of trees that would lead into the clearing. The silence of being so far away from civilization surrounded her and every thought became a prayer of thanks.

As she walked, the symphony of the forest played. It was a composition she couldn't hear unless she listened very closely. The sway and creak of the trees provided the melody, her feet pounded out a rhythm and even the uncluttered air contributed an indiscernible but necessary part to the whole.

Her thoughts returned to Keith. From all she could see, he was not drinking anymore. Yet there seemed to be parts of his life he kept a tight lid on. She had no idea where his faith was at or what had taken place that led to him coming back to the ranch.

Oh, God, tell me what I should do.

She took in a deep breath. Like a glass breaking, a clanging and whirring noise shattered the silence. A second later, lights flashed and rose slowly upward. The helicopter. Jenna dropped to the ground. Even though she lay flat on her stomach, this open area left her exposed and vulnerable. Inside the carrier, the owl's wings beat against the plastic.

The helicopter was close enough that she could make out the outline of the pilot's head though she couldn't discern any details in features. Another man perched in the open door holding a gun.

The copter hovered, then angled in her direction. The windows of the helicopter looked like giant bug eyes staring at her. She pressed harder into the ground. No matter what she did, the bright colors she always wore meant she would never blend in with her surroundings. Maybe dimming evening light would work in her favor.

The helicopter turned to face her. The cacophony of blades and motor drowned out all other noise. Her heart hammered against her rib cage and the adrenaline kicked in. She fought the urge to get up and run for the cover of the trees. A brightly covered moving object was a lot more noticeable than a motionless one. If she held still, she might get lucky, and the pilot and his gun-toting friend would be focused on the sky, not the ground.

The helicopter surged toward her. She took in a sharp, quick breath and pressed her cheek against the grass. Without even thinking, she had placed a protective hand on the carrier. Her other hand dug into the soft earth. The helicopter flew directly over her. Once it was on top of her, the noise made her feel like she had been pulled under by an ocean wave, losing all control of what happened next, at the mercy of the tug of the waves. She remained motionless, not even daring to take a breath, fearing that she had been spotted, fearing that it would turn back merely trying to get a better angle on her, fearing that its armed occupant would take aim at her and she would be able to do nothing.

At first the whirring of the blades remained strong, but then it slowly grew more distant, started to fade as the volume of the forest turned back up again. Even after she could no longer hear the whop, whop, whop of the helicopter, she remained immobile, her stomach pressed into the earth.

Still shaken, Jenna rose to her feet. Off in the distance, she could see the glowing light of the helicopter, though she could not hear it anymore.

As it had done before, the machine descended and disappeared for several minutes and then rose straight up.

Whoever was in that helicopter was dropping something off or picking something up at various locations. She had to find out what it was.

Jenna turned her attention toward the trees the helicopter had risen out of. She picked up the carrier and returned the traumatized bird to the back of the car, then double-checked to make sure she had her flashlight and her pocket knife. Even though logic told her these would not be viable weapons, they made her feel safer.

The helicopter had done its second drop at least three miles from where she was, as the crow flies. Chances were they weren't coming back. Still, taking precautions always worked to dispel fear. Having the knife calmed her jittering nerves. She felt a twinge of pain. If Keith had been here with her, she wouldn't have been afraid at all. He knew how to handle this kind of thing.

Jenna closed up the car and jogged out to where she'd seen the helicopter rise. It was the same place she had planned on releasing the bird. A large open area surrounded by a circle of trees. The soft earth revealed where the helicopter had come down. The feet of the helicopter had left deep impressions in the mud.

In the time since she had started her hike, the sky had turned from blue to gray. She turned on her flashlight and surveyed the area around the helicopter markings. She walked a full circle, finally locating a footprint. The helicopter's weight probably would have left an impression even if the ground wasn't soft. The footprints, though, were not as discernible. Where the ground was harder, they seemed to disappear altogether. By getting low to the ground and shining her flashlight, she was able to follow the path of the runner into the trees. Jenna stepped into the forest. Deadfall and accumulated pine needles made the ground soft, and the tracks were cleaner.

She shone her flashlight around a fallen log. Why would someone jump off a helicopter and run into the forest? Maybe they weren't dropping something off, maybe they were picking something up. If something had been left behind, she would find out what it was.

She took a few more steps forward, leaning so she could shine the light low on the ground. She spotted an impression in the muddy earth. The waffle pattern of tread from a boot materialized as she studied the forest floor. She ran her fingers over the tiny bumps and then shone the light in the direction the footprint pointed.

The footprint led toward a healthy evergreen that was separated from the other trees because of its hugeness. If someone was going to hide something, this tree would be a good marker. Jenna searched all around the tree and then shone her light upward. Nothing.

Disappointment spread through her. Maybe something had been stashed here and taken away. Then she noticed one of the branches was longer than the others, like an arrow pointing. She followed the direction of the arrow to a log.

Closer inspection of the log revealed that it had been cut along the top and hollowed out. Jenna lifted the cover off the log. She drew out a note with numbers on it, a canister with a set of keys in it and a pistol.

Jenna looked around. Even though she knew the helicopter was gone, finding the gun made her edgy. Thoughts of Keith bombarded her mind. This would have been less scary with him.

The sheriff would want to see these items, maybe even come up here. Her hand shook as she drew out the pistol. Guns made her nervous.

A tree creaked somewhere in the forest.

Jenna slipped the canister and the index card into a pocket of her vest. She held the gun at her side. Maybe there were fingerprints on these things. She headed back to her car, treading through the forest and out into the clearing. In the dim of evening, her car took on a dull shine differentiating it from everything else that was a natural part of the forest. Jenna placed the items on a piece of cloth and then put them into a box she had.

She should tell Etta and Norman King about this. She lifted her phone off her belt, but paused remembering that Keith didn't want to alarm his grandparents anymore than he had to. That meant talking to Keith first. She dialed his cell number.

"Hello."

"Keith, it's me, Jenna."

A moment of silence filled the line before he responded. "Hey, what's going on?" His voice sounded distant and guarded.

With some effort, Jenna managed a business-like tone. "I saw the helicopter on the ranch, and I found something hidden in a hollowed-out log about a mile from the double buttes. I thought you should know."

"Is the helicopter still there? Are you okay?" Concern colored his words.

"Yes, I'm fine, and no, the helicopter is long gone." A shiver ran down her spine. His concern was not unfounded. When they had been shot at before, it had probably been to scare them away from another cache that was being dropped. She'd been very lucky this time.

"What did you find?" His voice sounded shaky.

"Are you driving?"

"I just got done with a meeting in town. I'm headed back to Gramps's place. What did you find?"

"A gun, a metal canister with keys in it and a note with numbers written on it. I can't make heads or tails of it. Do you want to see it before I take it in to the sheriff?"

"I'll meet you up there."

"You might have trouble finding me. I am not even sure how far up the road I am. I can come down to you. Where are you?"

"I'm almost to the crossroads. How soon can you get here?"

"I've got to release a bird and then I can get right down there, probably in less than half an hour," she said.

"I can wait at the crossroads for you."

"Sounds good."

Jenna hung up. She pulled out the note card

and looked at it closer. Most of the numbers didn't make any sense. One sequence of numbers, 20-8, might stand for August 20, tomorrow's date. Keith might know what the other numbers meant.

Jenna pushed the box farther in her car and straightened her spine. More shadows were evident in the trees as the sun slipped down in the sky. Her heart skipped a beat; a chill climbed up her back. She turned, taking mental snapshots of each section of the trees. Her heart fluttered. This whole thing had stirred her up; made her feel like the forest was no longer a place where she could find serenity. She'd be glad to get down the road and out of here.

Jenna grabbed the owl's carrier again. A repeated thudding caused her to turn halfway. She caught a glimpse of face before an object slammed against her shoulder. Then, as she crumpled to the ground, a flash of metal revealed a car hidden in the trees.

She saw feet. The box with the items she'd found in the log being lifted out of the car. She stirred, digging her fingers into the cold muddy earth. She had to stop him. She tried to pull herself to her feet.

A second blow caused her world to go black.

* * *

Keith tapped his fingers on the steering wheel. Two intersecting roads stretched out before him. Only a wooden sign indicated that one road led to the King Ranch and the other to Craig Smith's place.

From the passenger seat where he sat, Jet craned his neck, resting his nose against his chest.

Keith checked his watch. "It's been half an hour." He let out a burst of air.

As if picking up on his anxiety, Jet whimpered and licked his chops.

She could have just been delayed with releasing the bird. Keith grabbed his cell and dialed her number. By the third ring, unease entered his awareness. He'd noticed that she usually kept the phone on her belt. After the fifth ring, urgency replaced concern.

Jet whimpered again.

"I agree, my friend." He rubbed Jet's head. "Let's go find her."

Somehow, he had a feeling that she wasn't on her way down the mountain. Anger at himself caused his muscles to tense. His hurt over last night had made him hesitate. He should have just headed up there when she called. So what if it was hard to find someone on that road. The last time they had encountered the helicopter, it had been right after they were shot at.

Keith started the engine of his truck and sped in the direction of the two buttes. There was only one road she could be on, but it was a long road. Finding her would be an approximation at best. Three times, he tried her cell phone. Tension suctioned around his rib cage.

Jet licked Keith's hand as if to offer comfort.

Keith stopped his truck at the first place he thought Jenna might release a bird. He jumped out of his truck and called her name. He hiked a couple hundred yards. No sign of her car. He'd have to keep working his way up the mountain.

By the time he was seated again behind the wheel, his heart was pounding a mile a minute. He could not bring himself to believe that something bad had happened to her...not now. Allowing that thought to come into his head would cause him to shut down completely.

When he had been in Iraq, his job as a combat medic required him to separate himself emotionally from the violence around him. He learned to process later. It was the only way a soldier could stay alive.

Where Jenna was concerned that was hard

to do. Even more so now that he had found out something about her. Jenna's rejection from the night before had left him feeling vulnerable, so he had located an AA meeting in town. Richard Murphy, Jenna's father, had been at the meeting.

Richard had shared with the group that he'd been sober for eleven months—beginning about a month after Jenna had stopped talking to him. Richard had left quickly after the meeting, only taking time to shake Keith's hand and tell him that he remembered him from years ago, but even their brief interaction had been enough to tell him volumes about why Jenna no longer spoke to her father—and why she'd turned away from him years before. If Richard Murphy had been drinking for all these years, that night twelve years ago made sense to him. His heart swelled with sympathy for Jenna. Of course his drinking scared her.

He took the anonymous in AA seriously. Without Richard's permission, he couldn't tell Jenna what he knew. The pain from last night's rejection had not gone away. His reaction to her voice earlier tonight told him that, but he saw Jenna in a new light now.

The truck wound up the rutty road, lurching over the bumps. The sky was dark gray the second time he got out to shout her name. Only the nighttime silence answered back. A mix of panic and despair spread through him. He had to find her.

He moved up the mountain at a slower pace, stopping frequently to study the landscape on either side of the road.

A car bumper entered the cones of illumination created by his headlights. Keith hit the accelerator and brought his truck alongside the vehicle. He jumped out of his truck. The car was a Subaru like Jenna's. He shone the flashlight into the windows. The contents of the car told him he had found Jenna's car. The doors and the hatchback on the car were shut but not locked. All four tires had been slashed.

He shouted her name, anxiety straining his voice. He stalked around the car making a wider and wider circle. Jet followed close behind. Keith reached down and ruffled Jet's head.

Keith opened the passenger-side door of Jenna's car and searched for something that might contain Jenna's scent. He located a sweater under the back of the driver's seat. Keith brought the sweater to his nose. Yes, that was the sweet lilac scent of Jenna.

Jet was not a trained search and rescue dog,

but it was worth a shot. He placed the sweater under Jet's nose. "Go find her, boy."

Jet jerked up his head and barked but remained close to Keith. "Go find her." He placed the sweater under Jet's nose again and then pointed. "Where is Jenna? Go get her."

This time, the dog ran in the direction Keith pointed. The same thing he did when Keith was tossing the ball for him. Keith shook off the creeping sense of hopelessness. Jet was a smart dog. It might work.

He continued to widen his search circle, working his way out toward the trees, swinging his flashlight across the ground. Had someone taken Jenna?

Again, he had to swipe the idea from his brain. He was no good to anybody if he played the "what if" game. Logically, he knew that if she was around here and conscious, she would have answered by now…unless she was tied up…or worse.

Keith swung the flashlight over the tall grass. Nothing. He would search for her all night and into the next day if he had to. He was not going to give up easily.

Jet barked twice. Keith lifted his head. The trees were more shadow than discernible evergreens. Jet bounded out of the trees, danced back and forth and then disappeared into the forest again.

Keith jogged in the direction Jet had gone. The dog's excitement could have been over a squirrel, but he had to check it out. As he got closer to the trees, he noticed an area where the ground was pressed flat as if something had been dragged over it. An icy cold washed over him.

His hesitation had put Jenna at risk. He would never let that happen again.

He ran faster. Keith saw a flash of bright pink. His light bobbed in his hand as he drew closer. He collapsed to his knees next to where Jenna lay on the ground, her legs twisted under her in an unnatural position.

Jet came back out of the trees. He licked Keith's face.

"Jet, go sit." The dog set back on his haunches, but his back legs quivered with anxiety.

Keith touched Jenna's face. Still warm. The throb of a pulse pushed back on his fingers when his hand trailed down her neck.

He shone the light directly on her face. She moaned. Dried blood crusted on her forehead. He gathered her head in his arms to try to find the source of the bleeding. Fresh blood streamed down her temple.

He tore the sleeves from his shirt and pressed one of them against her temple. It darkened with blood. He placed the flashlight in his teeth and angled her head. She had been hit, hard enough to knock her out. Rage coursed through him for what had happened to her.

Keith tied the two sleeves together and wrapped the makeshift bandage around her head. The bandage darkened. He pressed his face close to her lips. Her breathing was shallow, but still there. Keith lifted Jenna's eyelids, angling the light so it wouldn't shine directly in her eyes. It didn't look like her pupils were dilated. She hadn't jerked back when he shone the light in her face, so she was conscious but unresponsive. Keith stroked her forehead. Even though the color had left her cheeks she was as beautiful as ever. "Jenna, can you hear me?"

Come on, Jenna, answer me.

ELEVEN

A voice from very far away drifted into Jenna's awareness. What was going on? She felt like she was swimming through gelatin. The voice drew her upward. A deep bass voice whispered prayers. Was she dreaming?

"Please, God, let her be all right."

Warm fingers touched her cheek. With great effort, she opened her eyes. Keith gazed down at her with gentle gray eyes.

"Hey, there."

He had placed her sweater underneath her head. He'd taken such care with her. His prayer warmed her even more. Any man who would pray like that when there was no one but God to hear must have a deep faith. She tried to piece together what had happened. The moon above her told her that she was outside, but her brain felt fuzzy. What was the last thing she remembered?

She lifted her head, catching a glimpse of Jet who lay a few feet away.

Keith jerked. "No, don't do that."

Pain shot through her head. She moaned and lay back down. The throbbing lessened if she held very still.

Jet whimpered and licked her hand.

"You got hit pretty hard."

"Hit?" Ah, yes, now she remembered. "He must have come up here to get the stuff in that cache. The helicopter is for dropping the stuff." She winced and touched her shoulder.

"He hit you there, too." His touch on her shoulder was soft, but his voice was indignant at what had happened.

Jenna nodded. "I don't think it's bleeding, just bruised."

"Did you get a look at him?"

She couldn't think straight. "Kind of?" She searched her memory. She had seen him just for a moment. When she tried to picture his face, she drew a blank. Her temple pulsated.

"Don't worry about it now." His hand cupped her cheek. "I didn't want to move you in case there was additional injury. Can you feel your toes?"

She smiled. Now he was worrying too much. "Yes." His fussing over her was kind of sweet.

"Your legs were twisted funny. That's why I asked."

"He must have dragged me over here." She lifted her hands, touching the bandage. Just one more way Keith had taken care of her.

Keith nodded. "I should have just come up here right away. Anytime that helicopter shows up, it's bad news." His mouth grew into a tight line.

"I'm the one that said to meet me at the crossroads." She grabbed his arm. "I'm just glad you came." Her hand brushed over rough skin. He wasn't wearing long sleeves.

He jerked back, jumped to his feet and turned away from her.

"What happened to your arms?" She stared at his back.

"They're…scars." He placed his hands on his hips. "It happened in Iraq. When my whole life blew up in my face."

Somehow she had a feeling the scars were less about him being self-conscious and more about how they were a reminder of his life getting off course. No wonder he couldn't talk about the past. Despite the undulating pain, she lifted her head. Her heart swelled with empathy. "I have lots of scars, too. Most of which I got when we were out having our adventures." She struggled to keep her tone light, teasing.

"This is different, Jenna." He was still turned away from her.

"You got those in sacrifice to others…didn't you?" Her voice grew thick with sorrow for what he must have gone through. And she had thought the worst of him for covering his arms.

He bent his head, rubbing his forehead.

"I got my scars being stupid. Remember this one?" She sat up. The throbbing in her head made her eyes water. She lifted her pant leg. "I think this one happened when we were hiking. I collided with that sharp tree branch, remember?"

Keith remained with his back to her.

She rolled up her sleeve, brushing her hands over the area above her thumb. "I think this one happened when we built the tree house. I never was very good with a hammer."

"Jenna, it's not the same."

"I know." With substantial effort, she pushed herself to her feet. She wobbled and planted her feet. She stepped unsteadily toward him. When she placed her open hand on his back, he didn't pull away. "Yours mean something."

"I got off a lot easier than a lot of other guys. I'm still walking around."

The heat from his back seared through her hand. What had this man been through? Guilt washed over her for all the suspicions she had harbored about him.

He hung his head. "What bothers me is that I have a memory of what my arms used to look like." He turned slowly to face her. "That I used to be able to do things without pain."

She rested her open hand on the hard muscle of his bicep. Maybe his self-consciousness hinted at a deeper scar. Her fingers skated his arm to the crook of his elbow. With a soft touch, she traced his scar down his forearm to his wrist. With her other hand, she touched the other scar. "This doesn't bother me." She tilted her head. "It doesn't bother me at all."

Jenna's clear warm eyes held him in place. He searched for some indication that she was lying, just to make him feel better. The last thing he wanted was her pity. Her expression and the magnetic pull of her eyes communicated sincerity. Her fingers fluttered over his scars as light as wind. Her complete acceptance of him despite physical flaws caused him to let his defenses down. Her touch sent a charge of electricity straight through his skin to the marrow of his bones. With the back of his fingers, he traced the outline of her jaw.

He leaned closer, wanting more than anything to kiss her. But the memory of last night haunted him. He hesitated.

Jenna let out a gasp and stepped closer to him. Her hand rested against his chest. She locked him in her gaze. In her eyes, he saw that she would not hurt him...not like before.

He bent his head, brushing his lips over hers and then pressing harder. His hand trailed down her neck as she melted against him.

He pulled away. "I think I have wanted to do that for twelve years."

"Twelve years?"

"Never mind."

"I know what you are talking about. That night, right before your arrest. I was a brand-new Christian. My faith was fragile—everyone was telling me you were bad news. And the way you'd been acting all summer... You scared me."

He doubted that was the whole reason. "I see that now." He understood more than he could say. She had been so afraid that night twelve years ago because his behavior reminded her of her father. What was keeping her from sharing about her father now?

He longed to ask her more about her father...
to say what he knew, but that would have to wait.
How long had her father had a drinking problem? His heart swelled with sympathy. What a
heavy load for a kid to carry.

He touched his hand to his chest where his
heart raged against his rib cage. Some scars were
where everyone could see them and others were
invisible. The unseen wounds had driven many
of his choices. He saw now that he could trust
Jenna.

"We should probably get back down the
mountain, get you to the doctor and call the
police," he said.

Jenna's eyes grew wide. "The owl. Was the
carrier still beside the car?"

How quickly her thoughts turned to the birds.
He shook his head. "I think so."

She was already halfway across the field.
Keith sauntered behind her, still basking inside
the warm glow of the kiss.

Jenna had opened the hatch of her car. She
collapsed on the edge. "My head really hurts."

Keith rushed over to her. "Jenna, we need to
get you checked out at the hospital."

He noticed trembling in the hand she brought
up to rub the back of her neck. "I know that, but
this bird has been through enough. I've brought

him all the way up here." She gazed at him. "Can you help me? It won't take but a minute."

She wasn't going to leave unless they released this bird. Keith shrugged. "Sure. What do I have to do?"

Jenna burst to her feet, but swayed.

He grabbed her arms to provide support as she sat back down. "Maybe it's a good thing your car was disabled. For sure, I don't want you driving until we have you checked out."

Jenna furled her forehead. "That guy messed with my car." Irritation colored her words.

Keith pointed to the tires, and Jenna let out a groan. She tilted her head back but stopped midway, pressing her palm against the back of her head.

"You really need to take it easy." He brushed a hand over her silky hair. "I can probably find some replacement tires at the ranch. Gramps has plenty. Let's get you to a doctor."

"First, the bird." She crossed her arms, her mouth drawn into a tight line. She was not going to give up without a fight. He had to admire her tenacity.

"I'll take care of this. You sit right there. A head injury is nothing to mess around with. One day you're fine, and the next you can't remember how to find your way home."

"You know this from experience?"

"Yeah, I have seen it happen to some guys I was stationed with." He kneeled on the ground. "You've got to trust me on this one. I can let this bird out on my own."

"Okay," she relented.

"Just tell me what to do."

Jenna craned her neck from side to side. "It's not really hard. You just want him to have as little human contact as possible. Open the door and tilt the cage. He should be ready to come out. Sometimes, they don't take flight right away. As soon as he is out, back away as quietly as you can."

Keith reached beside the car, grabbed the carrier; his bare arm brushed against hers. She seemed to almost lean into his touch, a nice assurance that the scars really meant nothing to her. The back of his hand brushed over the smooth surface of her arm. "Goose pimples."

She rubbed her own arms and tilted her head as he straightened. "I know. I need to put that sweater on."

Without a word, he set the carrier down, retrieved the sweater and wrapped it around her shoulders. "Better?"

She nodded. Again, his gaze fell to her lips. He really wanted to kiss her again, to hold her

longer. To make sure the first kiss had been real.
Maybe later. He drew back, turning his attention
toward the carrier.

"I know it's dark, but you can't use a
flashlight."

"Not an issue for me. I am used to tromping
around in the dark."

"Something to do with your time in Iraq?"

Before, a wall would have gone up when she
probed, but now he found himself wanting to
share some of the details of his life. Some doors
still had to remain closed. Even he couldn't
revisit them, not yet. But for now... "Yeah, I'll
tell you about it sometime."

"I'd like that."

Jenna watched as Keith stalked out to the open
field. Her skin still tingled from his touch. The
light-headedness wasn't simply from the head
injury.

As he drew farther away, she could just make
out his silhouette. The moon provided only a soft
wash of light. He stopped and leaned over the
carrier to unlatch the door. He tilted the cage.
She saw a flash of white.

Jenna drew her knees up to her chest. The owl
had not moved since its initial escape. Inside her
head, she coached the bird.

Come on, little guy, take flight. You can do it.

Keith stood still, as well. Jenna touched her fingers to her lips. Though the kiss had been wonderful, it had left her feeling vulnerable. What happened now? At college, she had dated other men, but it had never gone beyond a few dates. Some of the men had been nice, solid Christian men. Some had only reminded her what a landmine relationships could be for her because she seemed to have radar for men like her father. With all those men, nothing had sparked inside her, even with the nice guys. Over the years, Keith had occasionally fluttered across her memory, especially in the summer. What if none of those other relationships got off the ground because she had met her soul mate when she was ten?

The thought made her heart beat faster as the strange mixture of excitement and fear flowed through her. Keith seemed open to sharing the parts of his life he had guarded before. That meant she had to let him into hers. Her back stiffened. Could she do that?

Keith took a few steps away from the bird. Jenna squinted, trying to separate the owl from the field. Owls do not make noise when they fly, one of God's special gifts that allows them to sneak up silently on prey. It did make it difficult, though, to tell if the bird had taken off. She waited for some flash of white in the moonlight. The standard policy was not to leave a bird until it showed it was capable of sustained flight.

Jenna rose to her feet. Keith increased his pace as he stepped farther away from where he had left the bird. He came up beside her.

"Did he take off?"

"Not yet." Keith stood close; the knuckles of his hand brushed against hers. His hand probed over her palm as he intertwined his fingers with hers. Her pulse surged. Delight at his touch and uncertainty about the future fought a war inside her.

She could barely discern the image of the bird taking flight. She pulled her hand away to point. "There, there he goes." The elation and feeling of victory flooded through her. This is why she loved this job. She turned to face Keith. His features were not discernible in the darkness.

"Kind of a good feeling, huh?" His voice was low and husky.

His kiss had turned her world upside down. She found herself longing to be in his arms again. Her head undulated, reminding her of her injury. She took a step back.

"Boy, do I wish I had an aspirin." She would

be able to think clearer and sort through things when her head didn't feel like it was about to explode. Then maybe she would know what to do about Keith Roland.

TWELVE

Keith eased the truck down the rutty dirt road.

Jenna sat close to him while Jet occupied the spot next to the window. The dog angled toward Jenna and licked her face.

Her laughter was like a soothing balm. "Do you think he's mad because I took his spot in the truck?"

"He'll get over it." Keith chuckled. The road flattened out, and they came to a more open area as they neared the crossroads.

Jenna yawned and rested her head against the back of the seat. "I am pretty tired. It's getting late. I'll call the sheriff tomorrow and tell him about what happened."

"Have you forgotten we need to have a doctor look at your head?" He was suddenly aware of his own fatigue. Maybe he would finally sleep well.

"I'm feeling a lot better."

"Jenna, don't argue with me."

Keith turned his attention to the dark road in front of him as it changed from dirt to pavement. In his peripheral vision, he saw movement right before metal crushed against metal. The truck was pushed sideways.

Jenna screamed.

Another vehicle with no headlights had come out of nowhere and crashed into the driver's-side door. Jet yelped.

The sound of squealing tires and a roaring engine surrounded them and then faded.

Jenna wrapped her arms around the barking dog, making soothing sounds. "What was that about?" Her voice intensified with fear.

Keith's heart raced. "I'll give you one guess." The truck had stalled out. He turned the key while the engine chugged but didn't spark to life. "If we can get this thing started, we are going into town tonight to tell the sheriff."

Jenna gazed all around them. "And…what if… we can't get it started?"

She was thinking the same thing he was, that someone was still out there, waiting for the chance to bash into them again.

He turned the key once more. The two vehicles hadn't hit the engine. "We'll get it started." The engine turned over and hummed to life.

He let out the breath he had been holding. He reached over and touched Jenna's cheek. "It's going to be okay."

He couldn't take the look of terror off her face, he could only get her to a safe place. He pressed on the accelerator.

Jet went into high alert stance, standing on all fours and barking. Keith increased his speed. Jenna's hand rested on his shoulder as she leaned into him. Jet turned on the seat, barking out the back window.

The old Dodge wasn't exactly a race car; its top speed was sixty. All the same, Keith pushed the accelerator to the floor. The lights of the town came into view.

"Almost there." He kept his voice level.

Jenna nodded, but didn't say anything.

Jet whimpered and settled back down.

"We'll go to the emergency room first."

He drove through town, past a dark bank building and general store. When he pulled into the parking lot of the tiny hospital, there were only two other cars in the lot.

Keith pressed against his door, but it didn't budge. "This side is smashed in. I'm going to have to get out on your side."

"They damaged it so much the door won't

open?" Though she was making a valiant effort, her anxiety was obvious.

He brushed a hand over her cheek. "You're safe here." Did he believe that himself? These people were relentless.

They scooted across the seat. Jet jumped out, pacing back and forth on the asphalt. Jenna got out next. She stayed close to the truck while Keith placed his feet on the pavement. Keith commanded Jet to get back in. He shut the truck door. Jet's face was barely discernible in the dark cab.

Jenna had grown quiet. It wasn't just her physical state he was worried about at this point. She was pretty shaken.

She hurried her pace and walked a few feet in front of him.

With a wary glance around the parking lot, he caught up with her and pushed open the glass doors of the ER.

"I'm so glad you are here." Her voice was faint.

A nurse bustled from behind a high counter and gathered Jenna into her arms. "Oh my goodness, Miss Murphy, what happened?"

"Long story," Jenna said.

The nurse addressed Keith. "You wait right here and Dr. Benson will have a look at her."

His makeshift bandages had come off her head, revealing the gash across her forehead.

Keith paced the hallway of the emergency room. If memory served, the rural hospital had only ten or so beds. If the doctor had any concerns about Jenna's condition, they would have to drive into Billings. A task he would be glad to do. She seemed okay…physically, anyway.

The nurse came back momentarily and settled behind the counter. "You've had quite a night."

Keith winced, suddenly aware of a pain in his shoulder.

"Are you okay?" She shot to her feet.

He must have banged against the door in the crash. "I'm fine."

The nurse stared at his scars. He pulled his arm back, but she grabbed his wrist. "I worked at a V.A. hospital when I was younger." Her voice was filled with compassion. "You don't need to hide those from me."

She was an older woman with salt and pepper hair and a sweet smile.

A lump formed in his throat. "Thank you."

She winked at him and then sat back down at her desk. "I am sure your girlfriend is going to be okay."

He didn't correct her on the girlfriend thing.

Actually, he kind of liked the idea of it. He tensed. His plan had been to leave at the end of the summer. He stopped and leaned a hand against the beige wall. He hadn't thought about the implication of the kiss when it happened. The desire to kiss her had been so strong. The fallout from it might be that he would end up hurting Jenna.

If the kiss had meant as much to him as it had to her, maybe he could change his plans.

"Do you have a newspaper?" he asked the nurse.

She pointed with her pen. "Yesterday's is over there with the old issues of *Field and Stream*."

Keith sat down and scanned the help wanted ads. Pretty scarce pickings where jobs were concerned, even if he decided to commute to a larger city. He tossed the newspaper back on the little table as frustration burned through him. This was total fantasy. What could he offer Jenna besides instability at this point in his life? He wanted to be with her. To take care of her. But he couldn't do that yet.

He rotated his sore shoulder. Pain shot down his arm.

"The doctor can look at that, if you want," the nurse said as she rose to her feet to clip a chart on a wall.

"I'm all right." Probably just some bruising.

He settled into an uncomfortable chair, resting his eyes.

Twenty minutes later, Jenna emerged from an exam room followed by the doctor, a middle-aged man in a brown cardigan.

"I am okay," she said. "I'm just going to have a bad headache for a couple of days."

The doctor pushed his glasses up his face. "A mild concussion. I don't think we are dealing with any long-term problems. She knows what to watch for. She needs to rest and no strenuous activity until the headache goes away."

After Jenna handed the paperwork to the nurse, Keith pushed the glass door open and held it so Jenna could step outside. It was dark. Most of the windows of the downtown businesses were dark.

"Are you up to telling the sheriff about what you found and what happened while we are in town?" Keith studied her for a moment. She looked better already.

"I'm up to it. The sheriff stays at his office pretty late. Let's go over there now."

The sheriff's office was in a side entrance to the courthouse. Sheriff Douglas sat behind a desk. A second desk was unoccupied. The sheriff hunched over a piece of paper. His left hand twisted unnaturally above the document as he wrote. He raised his head and tugged at his mustache. "Just the people I want to see."

"Really?" Keith stepped into the office behind Jenna.

"That blood sample from your door came back from the state lab. The good news is it's not human blood. Lab said it was consistent with canine blood."

"Canine blood? You mean a dog?" Jenna asked.

"Could be a dog, could be a coyote, could be a wolf. No one has reported the loss of a beloved pet. I've notified the game warden. He should be out of the hospital by the end of the week. If it was a wolf, it was shot out of season. Wolf hunts are very controlled and require a special permit."

Keith stepped forward. "Jenna found a stash of items just west of the two buttes."

Jenna summarized what had happened and ended by saying, "I only got a quick look at the guy, but his face wasn't familiar. Either he just moved to town or he is not from around here. I keep thinking, though, that I have seen him somewhere before."

The deputy came in from a back room and poured himself a cup of coffee.

"Was there anything distinct about him?" The sheriff rose from his desk while the deputy carried his coffee over to the second desk and sat down.

Keith placed his hand on the middle of Jenna's back. Jenna was a strong woman, but she had been through a lot in the last few hours. "It's all right if you need time to think about it."

"I'm okay." Jenna stepped forward. "My head started to clear when I was lying in the emergency room. He was pretty ordinary. Brown hair and kind of big nose." Jenna touched her own face as though she were trying to form the image in her mind. Then she put her hand on her chest. "The only unique thing about him was that he was wearing a necklace that looked like a piece of carved ivory."

"Anything else?" The sheriff picked up his coffee cup.

She shifted her weight. "This is kind of weird, but right before things went black, I smelled a strange smell. Not aftershave but a more earthy organic smell, really strong like—"

"Patchouli." The deputy scooted his chair back from his desk.

"Yes, that is what it was. I haven't smelled that scent since high school."

"I think I know who you are talking about."

The deputy pointed a stapler at Jenna. "Saw him a few nights ago at the Oasis bar. It's not an ivory necklace, it's a shark's tooth. He and four or five friends who weren't from around here were playing a lively poker game with some locals. They kept calling him Eddie. He was the only sober one in the bunch by the time the night was over. I stepped outside to make sure he was the one doing the driving. His vehicle was a candy apple red SUV, really distinct."

"We can call over to the Oasis and find out if he paid with a credit card. That would tell us his last name," the sheriff added.

"That is something, then," said Jenna. Her voice sounded faint. She squeezed her eyes shut and then opened them wider than usual as if she were trying to stay awake. The stress of everything and lack of sleep was probably starting to wear on her.

"Sheriff, if you want, later today, we can ride up to where it happened. I have to get Jenna's car anyway," Keith suggested.

The sheriff nodded.

Keith escorted Jenna out of the sheriff's office. They stepped onto the sidewalk. Jenna stopped for a moment.

"What are you thinking about?" Keith asked.

"I was thinking about how we have had an

unusual number of calls about bear carcasses. We get the calls because the turkey vultures show up for dinner. It's always just a partial carcass. The claws are missing, sometimes the head, sometimes the hide. I just assumed another wild animal had already helped itself."

"I think I follow you—eagles, wolves and bears. All illegal to hunt this time of year."

"Eagles you are never supposed to shoot," she said. "One or even two people couldn't do all that poaching. The vandalism at my place was done by at least two people. It was a large group up in Leveridge Canyon that night."

"So this isn't about smuggling. We are talking about a group of guys who hunt illegally, mostly at night."

Jenna rubbed her forehead. "I wish I could remember the numbers on that index card. I know there was one that I thought might be a date."

"Maybe you don't need to remember. What if we assume it was some sort of code? Maybe a longitude and latitude that told them where to meet. The cache provided a weapon and keys to a vehicle—probably a four-wheeler or a motorcycle—that they picked up at a different location."

Jenna stopped and stared up at the sky. "We

need to find this Eddie guy. Someone has to be organizing this. What if he is the one?" She touched the bump on her head. "The sheriff can charge him with assault and then ask him—" Her words trailed off.

She tensed as she peered up the street. Her father had parked his car and was making his way to his house carrying a stack of books. He stopped for a moment, aware that he was being watched.

Jenna waved. A look of sadness crossed his features and Richard nodded in response.

Keith studied Jenna for a moment. He read sorrow in her expression. "Aren't you going to talk to him?"

"A wave is enough."

"You guys don't have your noontime get-together anymore?"

"I'm a grown-up now, Keith." Irritation had entered her voice. "I don't need to discuss *Treasure Island* with my father."

From what he could tell, they didn't discuss anything. Richard's words at the meeting floated back into his head. The one thing Richard wanted more than anything was to restore his relationship with his daughter. He had a feeling that was what Jenna wanted, too. She didn't know that he had stopped drinking.

Keith knew enough not to push. This had to happen on Jenna's timeline. "Maybe someday, you'll walk over there and knock on that door."

"You think it's that easy?" Her words took on a defensive tone. "Things with my father had gotten really unhealthy. I needed to set some boundaries." Jenna's cheeks turned red.

"I can respect that."

Jenna twisted her hands together. Her tone softened. "It's just too hard."

"I understand." The anxiety he saw in her expression tore at his gut. But he would not manipulate the situation. This had to be Jenna's decision.

Richard passed by a window. Jenna took in a breath.

"I spent a lot of my life focusing on what I didn't have, a dad. I couldn't see that I had cool grandparents who loved me. I always thought what you and your father had was pretty special."

"My dad is special. He can be…wonderful." She pressed her lips together then turned to face him. "Keith, you just don't know the whole story."

"Try me." Was she ready to share?

She stared at the ground for a long moment, then tilted her head and blurted out, "My father has a drinking problem. Last year, it got so bad that he ended up in the emergency room." Her voice cracked. "I will not watch my father commit slow suicide. I have to keep myself healthy and not get caught up in his craziness. It hurts too much."

"What if he stopped drinking?"

"That has happened a bazillion times. He always goes back to it. I can't live through that cycle of becoming hopeful only to have that hope crushed again. If that makes me the world's worst daughter, then so be it."

"I would never think that about you. I can see how much you love your dad. And sometimes love means being tough."

She studied him for a moment. Her expression registered surprise, as if she hadn't expected him to say what he had said. Her eyes glazed. "That's what makes it so hard. If he was just a big fat jerk, I could walk away. I would have moved somewhere else after college."

He laced his fingers in hers.

"I do care about him." Strength returned to her voice.

"You'll know when the time is right."

"I think it is today." She squeezed his hand tighter. "Will you be the one to knock on the door?"

"Sure."

He led her across the street, and as he walked, each step was a prayer that he hadn't been out of line and made her feel pushed to do this. Time apart from someone with a drinking problem could be a positive thing for everyone involved, especially if it led to reconciliation. It had taken him twelve years to come back to his grandparents. He prayed that the outcome would be good for Jenna too. Her hand tensed in his when he lifted his free hand to knock on the door.

They waited for what seemed like an eternity. Footsteps crescendoed toward the door. Jenna squared her shoulders and straightened her spine.

The door swung open.

THIRTEEN

Her father's eyes widened when he opened the door.

Jenna planted her feet and fought the urge to run away. Her heart hammered in her chest. As if sensing her anxiety, Keith leaned closer to her.

The memory of the last time her father was in the hospital hit her like a punch to the stomach. As he lay beneath the blue hospital blanket, his skin had been almost yellow. Even in his sleep, his hands had been palsied. The words of the nurse on duty floated back into her head. "If your father doesn't stop drinking, he'll be dead in six months. He's done so much damage to his body already."

The warning echoed through her brain as she studied her father standing in the doorway. In the past year, Richard's skin had lost its sallow quality. He looked like he was getting a little sun. His eyes were bright and clear.

He said her name. "Jenna." He offered Keith a nod of recognition.

His voice pierced through her. Like an intense gust of wind, all the years of pain and secrecy hit her full force. If it hadn't been for Keith standing beside her, she would have turned around and walked away.

Keith cleared his throat. "Mr. Murphy, we thought we would come over and say hello."

Jenna almost laughed at the understatement. The need to laugh rose from nervousness. Keith spoke to her dad like they were old friends, which didn't make any sense. Maybe they had passed each other on the street and exchanged small talk, but she doubted they'd done any more than that. Keith hadn't been back in town that long.

Richard angled to one side. "You can do more than say hello."

They stepped inside. Bird cages containing finches and shelves of books filled the living room. The worn leather chair with the stack of novels beside it was still situated so the sun would warm it in the early morning. Her father had kept her papasan chair where she used to curl up to read. The plaid throw she covered herself with in the winter was flung over the chair as if he expected her to come home at any time.

The grandfather clock ticked away the seconds, punctuated with the chirping of the birds. The smooth voice of Frank Sinatra spilled from the radio in the kitchen. Her dad had always liked the Rat Pack crooners.

Jenna pointed toward one of the cages. "You've got a robin?" All the other birds were the domesticated species he had always had.

"Yes, that little girl who lives off Madison Street brought him to me. He got caught in some mesh that was put over a cherry tree to keep the birds from eating them."

She pointed to a cage that held a turtle dove. "Where is Maurice?"

Richard walked the few feet to the cage, opened the door and let the bird step onto his hand.

He brought the turtle dove over to Jenna. Her father cooed at the gray white bird. "I am afraid Maurice didn't make it through the winter." He tilted his hand.

Without thinking, Jenna lifted her arm, allowing the bird to transfer to her hand. "So Maureen is all by herself now." The thought of the turtle dove losing her lifelong partner caused a sadness to swell in her heart. The sorrow was so intense; she knew it wasn't just about the death of the bird. The bird fluttered its wings. Jenna's throat constricted.

Her father stood close.

"You look good, Dad." She had not intended to whittle away the time with small talk, but what really needed to be said was so difficult. Everything they were saying was coming out in code.

Her father took a step back and blurted, "I haven't had a drink in almost a year."

Jenna glanced toward Keith. "How did you know?"

Keith looked at Richard, who nodded. "I have been sober for twelve years, but every once in a while, I still need a meeting."

Had her father really joined AA? And stayed sober for a year? This was different than the other times. At most, his past sobriety lasted a week. A small seed of hope budded inside Jenna. She looked back at her father. "Why didn't you tell me?"

"I figured you would come to me when you were ready." Richard held his hand out for the dove. "I didn't want to hurt you again. I saw that look in your eyes in the hospital."

There had been harsh words between them.

Guilt had fueled much of her anger that night. If she had not kept his addiction a secret, thinking she was somehow protecting her father for so many years, maybe it wouldn't have gone this far. After a year apart, she understood that the responsibility to change was her father's.

The time apart had been good for both of them. All the anger she had wrestled with a year ago had dissipated.

He returned the bird to her cage. "Things are going so much better now." A sparkle flashed through his eyes and he raised his finger. "I want to show you something." He left the room, feet padding softly on the carpet.

Jenna mouthed a *thank you* toward Keith. Whatever the future held for them, Keith's gentle urging had led her to discover the change in her father.

Richard returned holding a stack of typed pages. "I'm writing again. My novel."

Her father hadn't written in years. When she was little, he had talked of writing a book. He would work on it in fits and starts and then Jenna would find the pages in the trash can or the kindling box. After that, she would catch her father flipping through photo albums, staring at pictures of her mother, usually with a drink in his hand.

"I even have a publisher who is interested."

"Daddy, that is wonderful." All of this was different. He wasn't trying to quit on his own. He was going to meetings. He was taking it seriously. And he'd done it for her. The tiny seed of hope inside her budded and pushed through the fragile earth.

"Some afternoon when you have time, I would love for us to talk through what I have written." He gripped the manuscript as excitement entered his voice.

"I'm not an editor or anything." Her father's enthusiasm made her smile.

"But you are a reader. You know a good story. I value your opinion."

The clock struck midnight. "You have to get to bed, don't you?"

Richard set the manuscript on a table. He grabbed her hand but then pulled away as though he had been too impulsive.

She took his hand in hers and squeezed it. "I will come by the next time I am in town."

"I'll make a big pot of tea."

Her father sounded hopeful, too. Maybe things could be repaired. That night in the ER, she had let go of her father, left him to die. She had felt guilt over that decision, guilt that came out in anger. In retrospect, they had been like two drowning people trying to save each other. Now they had a life preserver between them.

Richard held out a hand for Keith to shake. Keith pulled the older man into a back-slapping hug.

As they stepped outside, Jenna knew she had to be realistic. This time was different, but she still needed to be cautious about imagining a life with a sober father. She looked at Keith. He really was a different person.

The wild seventeen-year-old kid who had broken her heart and frightened her so much was gone. They crossed the street angling toward Keith's truck.

Jenna opened the passenger side door. "So did you totally give up on rock climbing when you left twelve years ago?"

Keith got into the cab and stuck the key in the ignition. "Pretty much, but I'd start it up again with you."

His smile sent shock waves through her. "You're the only person I trust to belay me."

Keith cranked the gear shift and hit his signal before pulling out into the street.

"I don't think I even have any gear still." She had gotten rid of everything that reminded her of Keith. She hadn't been climbing in twelve years. "I'd have to buy some."

His face glowed with affection. "We're both a little out of practice. I'm just starting to get some strength back in my arms."

Keith drove Jenna back to her house with the promise of bringing her car by later before he went out with his grandfather to spot cattle. Even though her head still hurt, Jenna felt lightness in her step.

She was okay with the kiss from Keith. She wasn't keeping secrets from him anymore. She was at a place of new beginning with her father. As she wandered to her house to get some sleep, Jenna found herself hoping for more kisses from Keith.

Keith turned slowly and stared down the path at his grandfather. The old man kept up pretty well. Keith remembered being a teenager and hiking this mountain with Gramps. Then, he was the one who had been challenged by his grandfather's huge strides.

Norman King peered out from beneath the rim of his weathered cowboy hat. "Don't go stopping on my account. We're burning daylight." Keith lifted his head and laughed, knowing they had hours before sunset.

Keith took the final few strides to the summit. They were nearly to the top of Cascade

Mountain, the highest point on the ranch which provided a panoramic view of the valley. If they couldn't spot the unaccounted for cows from here, the cows were really lost, and they'd have to hire out a search plane or helicopter.

Summer on a ranch was mostly about upkeep and repair. The cows were turned loose to forage for themselves on the abundant grass. Once the weather grew colder, the cows would be brought in and fed hay until they were ready to sell and ship to the Midwest for fattening in November. February and March were the busiest months because the cows they kept would be calving. Depending on where he found a job, he hoped to at least get back to help Gramps with the calving.

Keith took in a deep breath of thin mountain air. A marine friend had called him with a lead on an EMT position in Denver. The job would provide some additional support while he went to college on the G.I. bill. The summer had done the healing he had hoped for. Leaving had always been the plan. What he hadn't anticipated was a renewal of his feelings for Jenna. He still wasn't sure what to do about that. She loved working at the center and things had been patched up with her dad. For sure, she wouldn't be open to moving. Long distance relationships usually fell apart.

Keith put the binoculars to his face, searching for the moving black dots that were the missing Angus. When he had enlisted and been deployed, his ability to identify objects at a distance had turned out to be an asset in the desert. Because most people were used to being surrounded by buildings, their eyes were trained to see only short distances.

"Spot anything?" His grandfather came and stood beside him, huffing for air.

"Not yet." He handed over the binoculars to the older man. "You want to take a turn, eagle eyes?"

Norman lifted the binoculars, peering at one spot, turning twenty degrees and studying another area on the landscape. "Two of them at twelve o'clock." With a look of triumph, he handed the binoculars to Keith.

Keith focused the binoculars on the place where his grandfather had just looked. He stared until two distinct black dots separated out from their surroundings. "Well, how do you like those apples."

"The old man still has it, huh?" Norman slapped his grandson on the back. "Think they'll be okay down there?"

"They will be all right. There is a water hole over there."

"Small one. Might be dried up. We'll have to check it." His grandfather grew serious. "Keith, we sure have liked having you here this summer."

Keith pulled the binoculars away from his eyes. "You have no idea what it has meant to me."

Norman stroked his chin. "I can still wrestle a calf to the ground as fast as a man half my age." His bushy eyebrows shot up. "You know that."

"Sure."

"But just because I can doesn't mean I should. Etta would like to spend some time down in Arizona with her sister. The winters get kind of hard and long for her."

"Wouldn't you go a little crazy with nothing to do but sit in the sun?" He couldn't picture his grandfather in a Hawaiian shirt and white shoes and black tube socks.

"This isn't about me. It's about Etta. She's lived through all these winters without complaint."

His willingness to sacrifice for his wife was a testament to why their marriage had lasted so long. Keith had a feeling where the conversation was leading. "That would mean you would need someone to watch the ranch for you over the winter."

"Not watch. Run, yearlong. You're my only grandkid. After I'm gone to heaven, this place would be yours."

A lump formed in Keith's throat. "Gramps."

"That Peter Hickman has offered to buy it, but I don't like the idea of selling it off to a stranger. I want to be able to come back to the place and help out. I'd rather put it in more trustworthy hands." He cupped his hands on Keith's shoulder and squeezed it tight. "I know that wasn't what you planned. Take some time to think about it."

Keith's mind spun with what the offer meant. He couldn't imagine any better way to make a living. Ranching brought him a contentment he wasn't sure he could find anywhere else. Only one part of the picture was unclear. Jenna. They had both been operating on the assumption that he would be leaving at the end of summer. How would she feel about him if she knew he was going to stay around?

"Yes, I do need some time to think about it."

"We still have three unaccounted for heifers." Norman handed him the binoculars. "Earn your keep."

Keith turned toward the east, studying the lay of the land without the binoculars. In the distance, he could see Craig Smith's water tower and the road leading into Craig's property. "Where's the boundary for your property again?" Not that cows paid attention to any boundaries. Much of the ranch was unfenced. If the cows had wandered onto Craig's land and were eating his grass, it was Craig's responsibility to call and let them know.

Norman leaned close to Keith and pointed along a river and some lower hills. The vastness of the ranch had always taken Keith's breath away. He drew up the binoculars and scanned along the border between the two ranches.

A flash of red caught his eye. At this distance, it was hard to see what kind of car it was, but as far as he knew nobody but Eddie, the guy who hit Jenna on the head, drove a candy apple red SUV. The car was headed toward Craig's property. A car had to slow to about twenty miles an hour over that road. It would be at least fifteen minutes before Eddie arrived at his destination. Another car came into view from around a corner. Keith lifted the binoculars to his eyes.

A bubble of panic formed in his stomach. Jenna's car was closing in on the red car. What was she doing? They had no idea what they were facing with this Eddie guy. Other than that he'd already shown himself capable of assault.

"Come on, Gramps. We need to get down off this mountain." Keith explained what he had seen and the reason he was worried.

Norman rose from the rock where he had been resting. "We better get going, then."

The road down the mountain was winding and slow. Jenna would maybe get to Craig's place ten to twenty minutes before Keith could get there. He said a prayer for her safety. He strode down the mountain, mindful that he needed to allow his grandfather time.

Already his heart hammered in his chest. What was she doing trying to handle this on her own?

They arrived at his grandfather's truck. Keith's Dodge was still in the shop being fixed. Keith climbed into the driver's side and turned the key in the ignition. The engine purred to life. As the road evened out, he pushed the speed up to forty. Time seemed to stretch out. He wanted to go faster, but he would be no good to anyone if he put the truck in a ditch.

Jenna was smart, but if she thought Eddie had anything to do with the death of her eagles, she might throw caution to the wind.

Keith turned toward his grandfather. "Can you get cell reception?"

His grandfather pulled his cell phone out. "Yep. Looks like it's coming in good."

"Call the sheriff, fill him in and tell him to meet us at Craig Smith's place. And then try Jenna's cell."

After Norman completed the call to the sheriff, Keith recited Jenna's cell number.

His grandfather put the phone to his ear. Keith could hear the phone ringing over and over. Tension wrapped around his rib cage. When she was out in the field, she carried the phone on her belt. She should answer right away.

Come on, Jenna, pick up.

Norman pulled the phone away from his ear and shook his head.

FOURTEEN

Jenna's Subaru hit a bump, causing all her equipment to shake and rattle, but the car stayed on course. The new tires Keith had put on had nice traction. She watched the speedometer needle press past thirty. She had to get to Craig Smith's place fast.

She'd been headed back from a call about a bird stuck in a chimney when she'd seen the red SUV. The car had to belong to the Eddie guy who had knocked her unconscious and slashed her tires. Fortunately, the bird she had gone out to rescue had freed itself and flown away, so she didn't have to worry about jostling a bird in a carrier at these high speeds.

She had no intention of letting Eddie see her. Their last encounter had not gone well. There was a good possibility that Eddie didn't realize she could identify him, but it wasn't a chance she wanted to take. She really wasn't in the mood for another headache.

All she needed to do was make sure Eddie didn't leave and fall off the face of the earth. If she could get to Craig's first, she could talk Craig into detaining him. She stared at her phone. As soon as she had her reception back, she'd call the sheriff.

She pressed the accelerator. Craig would have a phone she could use.

She'd have to risk a possible car accident if she was going to get there before Eddie. The front wheels hit a patch of gravel which acted like a bucket of marbles sending her car into a swerve. Her heart raced even faster as she muscled it back onto the road.

How much time did she have? If she couldn't beat the red SUV to the ranch, she would just have to block the road with her car and hope she could reach the sheriff and get him out here before Eddie left. A much riskier solution.

She turned onto the road that led to Craig's ranch. No sign of the red vehicle in front of her and nothing in the rearview mirror, either. Strange.

Concerned, she slowed her car. At the very least, she should see a dust cloud created by his

SUV. She checked her phone again—still no service.

The water tower on Craig Smith's ranch came into view. She increased her speed until a flash of red in a ravine caused her to slow down. She pulled the Subaru over to a shoulder and braked. Jenna pushed open the door and trotted down the road. She shaded her eyes from the noonday sun and stared into the ravine.

Nestled in the junipers and boulders was the red car with its tail end pointed uphill. The car had left ruts where it had swerved off the road. She couldn't see Eddie anywhere. Fearing that he may be hurt and unable to move, she made her way down the hill, moving as fast as the steep incline allowed.

She slowed. What if this was some kind of trap Eddie had set for her? Maybe he had seen her car. She assessed the area all around her. Except for the boulders and junipers at the bottom of the ravine, the landscape didn't provide very many hiding places.

She walked faster again. She'd have to take that chance. She couldn't leave a hurt man alone in a car regardless of what he had done.

She trailed a hand along the side of the SUV. The front end of it had smashed against a rock, crumpling the hood. She drew her gaze to the driver's-side window. Eddie's head rested against it. He must be unconscious. She tried the door. It had been smashed in such a way that it wouldn't open.

Jenna raced around to the passenger side door. It was bent, as well. She darted to the back of the SUV, opened the hatch and crawled through. She scrambled toward the driver's seat, leary of what she might find.

"Eddie." He didn't stir. She leaned over the front seat. Fresh blood had stained the fabric. A pile of twenty dollar bills had spilled from an envelope and scattered. A coffee cup with the initials E.H. on it surrounded by a strange symbol sat broken on the floor of the car.

Eddie still didn't respond. Her fingers shook as she lifted them to his neck. No pulse. Paralysis set in as Jenna struggled for breath, encased in her own rapid heartbeat.

Eddie was dead.

She shook her head, fighting not to give in to the inertia that the panic caused.

She pulled Eddie's body away from the window. His shirt was soaked in blood. What could he have hit in a car crash that would make him bleed like that?

Her eye wandered to the smashed windshield.

Uneven concentric circles of crushed glass radiated out from a bullet-sized center.

Jenna backed out of the car as fear spread through her. Eddie had been shot. A million questions raged through her head, but it was hard to think clearly when she realized she had blood on her sleeves.

The breaking of branches and the crushing of undergrowth sent a new charge of terror through her. She stepped away from the car, her heart racing. The noise grew closer, louder. She was a sitting duck here.

Jenna leaped behind a boulder just as a cow emerged from the brush. The heifer wandered past her and back into the trees. Jenna whooshed out a breath and bent over.

She scrambled up the hill, falling twice and scraping her knee. Her shorts were ripped and she had blood on her leg. Her sleeves were stained with Eddie's blood. Unable to get a deep breath, she leaned against her car.

She pulled her phone out. Still no signal. She'd have to drive to Craig's place and call from there. Her hands were shaking uncontrollably. She lifted her head, staring at the high mountain and buttes that surrounded her. Maybe the shooter hadn't been close at all. What if Eddie had been shot with a long-range rifle from a high place just like the eagle? The thought that the killer might have been farther away gave her no comfort—with a rifle that powerful, she was still an easy target.

She couldn't think straight. She struggled to link one thought to the next one. It felt like her whole body was trembling from shock. Jenna took in a deep, prayer-filled breath and washed the images from her mind. All she had to do was think of the next thing she needed to do and then the next thing after that. She could do that.

She needed to calm down, so she could get in the car and drive to Craig's place and call the sheriff. She slipped into her vehicle and flexed her fingers on the steering wheel. She still felt like she was being shaken from the inside. She had just straightened her back when she glanced in the rearview mirror where a cloud of dust was visible. Someone was coming up the road.

Keith's breath caught in his throat when he saw Jenna's blue Subaru pulled off the road. He sped up the truck and turned off onto the first available shoulder. He jumped out and ran the short distance to her car.

The driver's-side door opened and Jenna

stepped out. There was a look of wildness in her eyes. She was in shock.

She pointed down the mountain. "Eddie… Eddie's been shot."

That didn't make any sense. They'd been operating on the assumption that Eddie was the one behind all of this. "Are you sure?"

"There is a bullet hole through the windshield." Her voice trembled with distress as she pulled away from him and ran a hand through her long hair.

First things first. He needed to keep Jenna from descending any further into shock. "Let's get you lying down." Gramps had already brought the truck closer.

Norman King met them halfway. "Jenna, what has happened?"

"She's going into shock," Keith said. "Can you grab that blanket out of the cab, Gramps? She can lie down in the truck bed."

The older man ran ahead, grabbed the blanket and brought the tailgate down.

When they got to the back of the truck, Jenna pulled away. "I don't need to lie down."

Keith cupped her face in his hands. "Listen to me—you are in shock. We need to get blood back to your vital organs. Okay?"

"You're the medic." A little bit of resistance colored her tone.

He led her to the rear of the truck and helped her crawl in. She lay back; the look of trust in her eyes floored him. Something deeper than friendship was growing between them, a bond that could weather a struggle. He pushed a tool-box across the metal of the bed. "I'm going to elevate your feet." He hooked his hands under her ankles. He touched the bloody knee. "Got a boo-boo there, huh?"

"Is that medical jargon?" She laughed. "I did that one." She glanced again at the blood on her sleeve, which made her shake her head and close her eyes. "But that isn't my blood."

His hand brushed over her temple, pushing her hair away from her face. "Don't think about it, Jenna."

She turned her head to the side.

"I found this in her car." Norman handed him a coat. Keith took the coat and laid it over Jenna. It tore him apart to see her so emotionally distraught. If only he had gotten here sooner. "Take some deep breaths."

Jenna locked onto Keith's gaze and breathed in and out.

She visibly calmed. He spoke to his grandfather who was resting his elbows on the side o the truck bed. "Keep an eye on her. I'll be right back."

Keith glanced up and down the road. A man on a tractor was coming from the direction of Craig's ranch, but still no sign of the sheriff.

Keith trotted back toward the accident site. He studied the damage to the windshield of Eddie's vehicle. It did look like a bullet had gone through the glass. He peered inside the car. Eddie was slumped against the steering wheel. The glove compartment had been thrown open in the crash. Maybe that was where that money had come from. A broken coffee cup with a strange symbol and the initials E.H. on it indicated that the car may have rolled or at least hit something with substantial impact before coming to rest against the rock.

When Keith returned, Jenna was sitting in the truck talking to his grandfather. Craig had parked his tractor a ways down the road and was walking toward them. The tractor looked new. Hadn't Craig said he was strapped for cash?

Keith grabbed the first aid kit from his truck.

Craig came beside the truck. "What's going on here?"

"Was a guy from out of town named Eddie coming to see you?"

Craig's expression darkened. "Why?"

Keith sauntered toward Jenna and his grand-father. Craig followed, stopping when he saw the wrecked car at the bottom of the ravine. His mouth dropped open.

"Is that his car?"

"He had…an accident." Keith elected not to tell Craig all the details.

"Is he—" Craig was visibly shaken.

Keith nodded. "At this point, the road leads directly to your ranch. There is no place to turn off and go anywhere else. Was he coming to see you?"

"I have never met the guy." Craig's tone was clouded with defensiveness.

Keith was pretty sure Craig was lying. He opened the first aid kit, pulling out disinfectant and a Band-Aid.

Craig took a step back. "Look, I got work to do."

"Sheriff will be here in a minute. This happened on your land. He might want to talk to you."

Craig drew his mouth tight. "If he wants to talk to me, I will be waiting at my place." Craig strode to his tractor.

Keith shook his head. Something was up with Craig. Why would he bring the tractor out if he was just going to turn it around and take it back to his place…unless he wanted it to look like he had casually happened upon the accident?

Keith held up the Band-Aid for Jenna to see. "For your boo-boo." Once Craig was out of ear-shot, Keith said, "He said he never met Eddie, but I don't know."

Jenna scooted to the edge of the tailgate. "He seemed nervous. I think I remember where I saw Eddie before. He was talking to Craig at the fundraiser."

"Really?" Keith squeezed out some disinfectant onto Jenna's knee.

"Yeah, they were having a heated discussion."

"Wonder what was going on?" Keith gently placed the bandage over her knee. "Better?"

Her smile shot a burst of heat through him. "Much," she said. She glanced toward the ravine. "It all feels…so surreal."

Combat hadn't made him immune to the impact of death, but he was probably better equipped to handle it than the average person. He brushed Jenna's soft cheek with the back of his hand. "It's never easy."

She closed her eyes as if gathering strength from his touch.

After opening her eyes, she jumped off the

tailgate and grabbed her coat. "I thought finding Eddie would answer questions, not create more."

The sheriff's car came into view.

"We don't know for sure if Eddie was shot. Let's wait and see what the sheriff can find out."

Jenna crossed her arms. "Maybe we had it wrong. What if Eddie was just one of the hunters?" She stared up the road where Craig's tractor was still visible. "Someone else must be organizing all of this."

It did make sense that a local, someone who knew the area, would be the one dropping the caches and setting things up. He was probably charging the hunters a lot of money. Maybe Keith had not allowed that thought into his awareness because somehow it made it easier if it was an outsider who was doing all this. He hadn't wanted to believe that one of his neighbors was a criminal of this magnitude.

Jenna placed her hands on her hips and stared down the ravine. "The sheriff is going to have to get a tow truck out here."

Jenna seemed to have recovered from the shock of finding the body. "Are you doing okay?"

She rubbed her bare arm and let out a shaky

sigh. "As much as I can be." She shivered. "I'll be all right. I just need a little time."

Keith wrapped a protective arm around Jenna. If Eddie had been shot these crimes had gone to a new and frightening level.

The sheriff stopped his car and walked toward them.

Jenna brought her car to a stop outside her father's house. A flutter of anticipation zinged through her. She grabbed the stack of books she had already read that she thought her father might like. It was Sunday. The library was closed. She knew she would catch her father at home after she finished church.

The events from yesterday still weighed heavily on her. The sheriff had confirmed that Eddie, whose last name was Helms, had been shot, but the shooter was still at large. Yet worship had left her feeling renewed and the thought of reconnecting with her father lightened her step.

Jenna pushed open the car door and stepped onto the sidewalk. She rapped gently at the door. The windows were open, and she could hear birds chirping and music playing. She knocked again, a little louder. She hadn't called ahead to let him know she was coming.

Maybe he was writing with his headphones on

and couldn't hear her. She turned the doorknob and stepped inside.

"Dad?"

No one was in the living room. She followed the sound of the music into the kitchen. The laptop was open on the counter. Jenna felt a little twinge of panic. What if her father had had a heart attack? She would never forgive herself for the year of silence if it ended like that.

She stepped onto the sun porch and breathed a sigh of relief. Her father, with his back to her, was staring out the window.

"Dad?"

He didn't turn around. She took a few steps toward him.

He spoke to the window. "I heard from that editor. They don't want my book."

"Oh, Dad, I'm so sorry. There will be other publishers."

He turned slowly. Shame clouded his expression. He held a glass in his hand. She recognized the amber liquid.

Jenna shook her head. Reality hit her like an icy gust of wind. This time was supposed to be different. Why had she let herself become hopeful? Her throat constricted, and her eyes warmed with tears. It was all a lie. People can't change.

Jenna turned and ran through the kitchen, out through the living room and back to her car. She fumbled with her keys, wiped her eyes and started the engine. She glanced at the door, thinking that maybe her father would come after her. She gritted her teeth. Why couldn't she let go of the idea that she could have a relationship with him?

She peeled out onto the street. Jenna drove for miles on country roads, losing track of where and when she turned. Thoughts charged at her from all directions. Anger and pain mixed together.

So what if some publisher didn't want his book? He was just looking for an excuse to drink. He probably wasn't even being honest about how long he had been sober. Lies, it was all lies.

She drove back to the center. She rested her head against the back of the car seat. She had no more tears left and no strength. She gripped the wheel. Why had she opened her heart to Keith? He was just like her father. It was probably just a matter of time before he drank again, too.

She closed her eyes and let her hands rest at her side. Every time she saw her father on the street, she would feel the pain all over again. Only now it would hurt even more. Keith had made things worse, not better.

Keith had been pleased to see Jenna's car pull into the center just ahead of him, but he was surprised when she didn't get out of the car. Stepping around to the driver's-side door, he tapped on her window.

Something about Jenna seemed off to Keith as she rolled down the window. There was a tightness to her features as if she were trying to hide something.

"What are you doing here?" Her voice sounded hoarse.

"I was just out driving and thinking after I went to early service at church," he said.

"What were you thinking about?" He caught a flash of anger in her voice.

Keith stepped back from her car. Something was definitely bothering her. "I was thinking about Eddie."

She opened her car door. He ambled back to his truck which now had a door a different color from the rest of the truck. He grabbed the piece of paper where he'd drawn the symbol he'd seen on Eddie's coffee cup. The sheriff had taken note of it but didn't think it was important. Keith hadn't stopped thinking about the symbol since he had seen it.

"This has to be a corporate logo or something."

She jabbed her finger at the piece of paper. "Didn't the sheriff say that Eddie's last name was Helms? The coffee cup has his initials on it—E.H." Her words were clipped, communicating impatience.

"Yeah, but what is with the weird symbol?"

"The sheriff will figure it out." Jenna pulled the keys for the center out of her purse. "I still have to do rounds with the birds. We don't have any volunteers come in on Sunday."

"I'll help you."

Her posture stiffened. "I can handle it, thanks."

Her coldness was confusing. Had he said or done something to upset her? "I want to help."

"Suit yourself." She shoved the key in the lock and twisted. The door swung open. "I just need to make sure there is no drama taking place with any of the birds and that they all have food and water. Everything else is paperwork I have to do on my own."

"We start here?" Keith asked, pointing to the birds next to the office.

She nodded. "Then the flight barn, then

the education birds. Pretty simple." They both reached for the doorknob at the same time. Keith's hand brushed over hers. She pulled away and offered him an icy stare.

"Jenna, what is going on?"

"Nothing is going on. I'm tired and I need to get this work done." He detected a subtext of hurt beneath her words. No amount of probing on his part would get him a straight answer. Asking her directly just made her more bent out of shape. He wasn't a mind reader. Whatever was going on, it was her responsibility to tell him.

Eight of the ten cages next door to the office were occupied. Keith checked four of the cages, dealing with two spilled water dishes.

Keith trailed behind Jenna down the hill to the flight barn. She lifted the board and slid the door open. She turned to look at him. The icy veil over her wide brown eyes was like a stab to his heart. "I'm really used to doing this alone."

Was she rejecting him again? He took a step back. The coolness and calm of late summer in the mountains surrounded him. Here they were again at a crossroads. Was he staying in Hope Creek or not? He needed a clear answer from her. "I've got a job offer driving an ambulance in Denver that starts in the fall."

A shadow seemed to pass over her features. She offered him a single word response. "Oh."

"So do you think I should take it?" Anxiety wove through him as he waited for her to respond.

She turned away from him, resting her hand on the frame of the door. He traced the outline of her long slender fingers with his eyes. Her hair took on a golden sheen in the afternoon sun, and he longed to touch it.

She angled toward him. Her eyes drew him in, but then she dropped her gaze and kicked at a rock on the ground. "It's your life, Keith. It always has been."

And she didn't want to be a part of it. She had made that pretty clear. He had his answer. "If you are used to doing this job by yourself, I will leave you to it."

She didn't look at him, didn't say anything, only gulped in a sudden shuddering breath before stepping inside the flight barn.

Inside the barn, wings fluttered, harmonizing with Jenna's soothing voice. Keith turned quickly and strode up the hill. Each step felt like a hammer blow to his heart. He and Jet could be packed and on the road by late afternoon tomorrow. The goodbye to his grandparents would be hard. His tie to them was the only thing holding him here. All other ties had been cut.

Jenna stood beside the open flight barn door and listened to the sound of Keith's Dodge starting up and fading into the distance. She stood for a long time, allowing the silence and loneliness to envelop her. Tears warmed her cheeks.

He had asked her straight out what was bothering her. Why couldn't she share what had happened with her father? Why hadn't she just told him about her fear that he would start drinking again? She had grown up in a home where she learned to talk around a problem, never stating anything directly. It was such an easy habit to fall back into.

She had nearly doubled over with pain when he had talked about leaving. She'd known all along that was the plan. But then hope had glimmered once again in her heart in the most cruel way. Even though they hadn't talked about it, after the kiss, she thought maybe things would be different...more permanent.

She should be happy. His leaving solved her problem and insured that the unbearable pain would not come again into her life.

She loved Keith. She knew that much. But being with him had the potential to bring so much hurt back into her life. With her father and with Keith, to open her heart was to risk being hurt. She had to let both of them go.

FIFTEEN

Jenna's cell phone rang just as she had tethered the bald eagle she was training to a post. Greta fluttered her wings and settled down. Jenna's mind was fogged from lack of sleep. She had stayed up most of the night thinking about Keith. It had been a long night and an even longer day. She pulled the phone off her belt and mustered up her best professional voice. "Hello. Bird of Prey Rescue Center, how may I help you?"

"This is Marybeth Helms. I'm Eddie Helms's wife." After a long pause on the other end of the line, Jenna thought she heard a sob. "The sheriff said you found my husband. He thought it would be okay if I called you."

"Yes."

"Was he alive when you found him? Did he say anything?" Even though Marybeth Helms chose her words carefully and spoke slowly, Jenna detected pain embedded in each syllable.

Jenna paced a few feet away from where she had tethered the eagle. This close to the flight barn, she had a nice view of the mountains. "I'm sorry, Mrs. Helms, but by the time I got to him…"

"I understand. I guess I was just looking for some closure, for an explanation."

Jenna stopped pacing and pressed the phone harder against her ear. "An explanation?"

"Eddie loved to hunt and find a new challenge with his hunting. He had done African safaris. We went to Alaska. I don't know what happened up there in Montana." Marybeth let out a faint cry.

"If this is too painful…"

"I want to talk. This last trip was different. He was afraid about something. He said things had gone too far."

So Eddie had been killed because he was going to blow the whistle.

"Did Eddie ever mention knowing someone named Craig Smith?"

"No…he never said any names." Silence filled the line for a moment. "He didn't talk much at all these last few months. My happy-go-lucky husband who loved the outdoors became this dark, brooding person."

"He felt guilty about something?"

"You know, the last time he got ready to go up to Montana, I remember thinking that this nightmare would be behind us." Her voice faltered. "And I would have my husband back." Marybeth sniffled.

Jenna could hear shuffling, water running, footsteps. Then she heard Marybeth talk to someone in the tone a person uses with a child. What could she say to comfort this poor woman? She said a quick prayer for guidance.

The hum of a car engine pulling into the center parking lot caught Jenna's attention. From where she stood, she couldn't see who it was.

"I need to go. I've got to go help my daughter. You've been very kind," Marybeth said.

With a heavy heart, Jenna said goodbye and hung up. Whoever had pulled into the center would have to come looking for her. She couldn't stop training. For a brief moment, she had wondered if it was Keith. Jenna shook her head. She had to let go of that hope.

She untied the eagle and set her on the fence post. "All right, Greta, let's try and get this right." She adjusted the glove. Greta had recovered enough for Jenna to start working with her. She would make a good education bird if she was responsive to training. Eagles with her wingspan were always a crowd pleaser, but she couldn't take Greta into schools if she was unpredictable. "You got to quit being such a teenage brat, okay?"

The bird tilted her head as though she understood.

Jenna offered the bird her gloved hand. "Up." Greta mounted onto Jenna's arm, rebalancing herself by flapping her wings. Even through the glove, Jenna could feel the strength of the eagle's talons. No matter how long she worked here, she couldn't become complacent about the kind of power she was dealing with. The dual ratcheting system of the talons that allowed this raptor to clamp down on its prey could just as easily dig into her. Eagles this size could topple a small deer if they wanted to. "Good." She pulled a treat from her pouch and offered it to the bird. "You like that part, don't you?"

"Ho, there." Peter Hickman waved at her from the top of the hill.

She signaled for him to come down. This would be a good test to see if Greta could keep her cool around another person. The bird shifted slightly on the glove.

When he arrived at the bottom of the hill,

Peter waved an envelope in front of her. "I've got some post gala donations for you. Some people just need a while for their hearts to soften."

A tinge of pain rolled through her at the memory of her time with Keith at the fundraiser. How long would it be before this didn't hurt anymore? She forced a smile. "Peter, that's wonderful—we'll be able to get a security system and knock off some of that other stuff from our wish list."

"So you are serious about that security system." Peter's mouth twitched. His smile seemed forced. "That sounds terrific."

Greta flapped her wings as though preparing for takeoff. Jenna could feel air moving from the force of the wings. She held the tether a little tighter. "I got to get this bird inside. She's still a little nervous around people."

"I would be glad to help."

"I can just put her in the flight barn for now. Then we can go to the office. I assume the people want receipts for their donations."

Peter chuckled. "People like the tax write-off." He sauntered ahead of her, unlatched the flight barn door and pushed it open.

Jenna stepped into the barn. A red-tailed hawk sat on a perch post close to the door.

Peter came up behind her. "You seem preoccupied."

She turned to face him, but took a step back because he was standing so close. He narrowed his eyes and tilted his head.

She was preoccupied...about a lot of things. She wasn't about to tell Peter about Keith, though. "I'm sure you heard about the shooting?"

"He nodded. Murder doesn't happen that often around here. The whole town is buzzing."

"Eddie's death is so disturbing. I just talked to his widow. I think he was trying to do the right thing. I think someone was making money off him and other out-of-state hunters, organizing these crazy illegal hunts."

"Oh, really?"

"Your place is right next to Craig Smith's. Have you seen anything?"

"Seen anything?"

Jenna shook her head. "I don't want to point fingers." She untethered the eagle and positioned her on a post. "But if you've noticed anything strange, like a helicopter parked on his land..."

Peter shook his head.

"You want to give me a hand? I need to take this guy in for a dose of antibiotics." She pointed toward an owl sleeping on a shelf by the windowsill. "If you could stand in the door and kind of block it, there is less risk of escapees. They are usually not that bold, but that red-tailed makes me nervous."

"Sure."

After attaching a tether, Jenna maneuvered the owl onto her gloved hand. The owl barely stirred. She strode over to the door. Peter stepped to one side so she could get out.

When she turned around, Peter was struggling to close the door. "It sticks sometimes. Give it a hard push."

He lunged at the door, and it slid into place. While he put the board into the hooks, Jenna noticed his keys had fallen on the ground. She leaned and picked them up with her free hand. Ice froze in her veins. Peter's key ring had the same symbol with the letters E.H. that had been on Eddie's coffee cup.

Peter turned to face her. Jenna managed a smile. "You dropped these."

He took the keys. His fingernails scraped across her palm. "Thank you."

Jenna's mouth went dry. "Why don't we head up to the office and get those receipts written up?" *And then you can be out of here, and I can call the police.*

"Everything all right, Jenna?"

Her heart pounded out a wild erratic beat. "I'm just shook up. Thinking about what happened to that poor man." She could tell that her voice sounded thin, like she was forcing the words out.

Peter offered her a smile. His teeth shone white in the sunlight. "The whole community has been shattered by this. It will be a while for healing to happen. I am thinking about opening up my home to the people in town, have some sort of get-together to help people process their feelings."

"I am sure the churches will do that, Peter." She struggled to keep the trembling out of her voice.

The owl flapped his wings, matching the rhythm of her own heartbeat. Her skin felt clammy.

Jenna turned and headed up the hill toward the office. The owl flew off her arm and landed on the ground. He bounced a few feet away from her. She raced after him, and he skittered a few feet more. Finally, she stopped him by stepping on the tether.

Peter materialized beside her. She could feel the heat of his body as he pressed against her arm. His fingers pinched the back of her neck.

"I think you and I need to go for a ride." He dug his fingers deeper into her nape.

The nerves in her neck muscles flared with pain. She gasped.

He spoke into her ear; his breath seared her skin. "But first, let's go to my car to get my gun."

Keith readjusted the suitcase on the seat of his truck as he drove through town. His goodbye to his grandparents had been bittersweet. He didn't deserve to be loved like they loved him. He could never repay them for what they had done for him. He would come back when he could to help out and to take care of them. Of course, that meant he might run into Jenna. The thought of even crossing paths with her made his chest ache.

Jet whimpered and rested his chin on the suitcase, staring up at Keith. They were nomads again. The lead on a job in Denver looked promising. He would land somewhere. He always did.

He parked and stared at the library as a young woman entered, holding the hand of a blond boy. The boy wasn't more than two feet tall and each step was a stretch for his tiny legs.

He had one more goodbye before he drove out

of this place. Keith stepped out of his vehicle and strode across the street and took the library steps two at a time. He wove his way through the stacks, past a group of moms sitting in a circle with their children while one of them read aloud.

Richard Murphy's silver gray hair was visible above the high counter of the check-out desk. He smiled and lifted his chin when he saw Keith.

Richard sat at the computer, clicking through pages that were mostly text. As always, there was sadness in his eyes despite the smile. Richard focused on the screen as he spoke. "I hear you are headed out of town."

"I came to say goodbye and to wish you well with everything."

Richard swung his chair around to look up at Keith. The sadness in his eyes intensified. "Everything?"

Keith nodded, wondering what the older man meant by the one word response.

Richard managed a smile. "Your support has meant the world to me."

Keith rested his elbows on the counter. Beside him were a pile of children's books ready for check-in. The top book was about wolves. Keith stared at the cover photograph, a black wolf with intense yellow eyes.

He would be leaving Hope Creek with a lot of loose ends. Things with Jenna had ended so abruptly, so coldly. Maybe there was one thing he could resolve or at least help bring to a close. He brushed his hand over the picture of the wolf.

"Can we do a little looking around on that computer?" Keith grabbed a piece of paper and drew the logo he had seen on Eddie Helms's coffee cup. "Can we find out what this means?"

Richard took the piece of paper. "We can give it a try." Richard retrieved another chair for Keith.

Keith settled into the hard plastic chair while Richard studied the drawing. "What do you think it is, anyway?"

"I was thinking maybe it was some sort of corporate logo?" Keith examined his own crude drawing and tried to remember what the original had looked like.

Richard scratched his head. "Maybe some kind of club symbol like 4-H."

Keith chuckled. "I don't think these guys were into raising pigs for the county fair."

Richard released a soft laugh. He paged through several websites. "I'm not finding anything." He turned his attention back to the drawing, tapping his finger on it. "E.H." He repeated the letters three times.

"I think that stands for Eddie Helms. But it is the symbol that is bothering me. Maybe we are making this harder than it has to be. Why don't we see if Eddie Helms had a Facebook page?"

Richard clicked through until he found the Eddie Helms they were looking for. There were pictures of Eddie on a boat with his wife and two children. Pictures of Eddie at the motorcycle shop he owned.

"This symbol reminds me of a crossbow," Richard said.

Keith studied the pictures closer. There was one of Eddie standing over a lion carcass he had just shot. He was wearing a T-shirt with the crossbow logo, and the letters E.H. Several men stood beside Eddie while others milled around him. Some were unaware of the camera and others offered a thumbs-up. They were all wearing identical shirts. Keith leaned closer to the computer, studying the photograph. His attention was drawn to a figure in the background of the image.

Richard touched the photo Keith was examining. "Looks like someone went on safari. That's some high risk hunting if you ask me."

"Yeah, high risk, very extreme." Keith shifted

in his chair. Now everything made sense. "E.H. doesn't stand for Eddie Helms, it stands for Extreme Hunters. I suspect that this guy is the club president." Keith pointed to a blurry figure in the background turned slightly away from the camera. "Peter Hickman knew Eddie Helms."

"They hunted together in Africa," Richard said.

Keith scooted his chair back. "I am going to tell the sheriff. Can you call Jenna and tell her for me?" It would be too heartbreaking to hear her voice.

A shadow fell across Richard's face. "I'm afraid my daughter isn't talking to me again and with good reason."

"But I thought—"

"Jenna came to visit me. I had gotten a letter from my potential publisher and waited until Sunday to open it. To celebrate the bad news, I had poured myself a drink. Guess I just wanted to feel it in my hand. I called my sponsor right after that. He assured me that this happens to everyone and I'm back on track, but none of that matters to Jenna. She is tired of being hurt by me, and I don't blame her."

"When was this?"

"Yesterday."

Keith's mind raced as he replayed his conversation with Jenna. "Sunday morning?"

Richard nodded.

Now he understood why she had been so cold to him. Seeing her father relapse had probably brought back old fears. She might have even blamed him since he was the one who had suggested reconciliation.

Richard gathered up the books off the counter. "For years, I could not see things from her perspective. She had to handle a lot as a child. I was too busy feeling sorry for myself to take care of her. Alcohol makes you selfish. I have put my daughter in the line of fire one too many times. Her hope has been built up, and I have dashed it to pieces."

"Do you want things to work out between you and your daughter?"

"More than anything." Richard's shoulders hunched. "But I wouldn't blame her if she never talked to me again."

"Don't give up, then. Sometimes you've just got to take these baby steps."

Keith's heart hammered in his chest. He had to find her, had to reassure her. "Why don't you take this information over to the sheriff? I think I am the one who needs to talk to Jenna."

Keith raced out of the library and across the

street. He jumped into the cab of his Dodge. Jet yipped at him. "All is not lost, my friend." Could he promise Jenna that he would never drink again? No. But he knew with God's help, there was very little chance of it.

The truck charged to life, and he pulled onto the street. Fear mixed with excitement as he turned off the city street onto the country road. Now that he understood how afraid she was of having to relive the loneliness of her childhood, would his assurances be enough?

The top of the flight barn came into view and he accelerated. He could call her cell and let her know he was on the way, but no, this needed to be done face-to-face. Explaining over the phone wouldn't work, and it might make her not want to see him at all.

He pulled into the center lot and jumped out of his truck. A Lexus was parked in the lot. A hush had descended on the center. When he tried the door of the center, it was open. He stepped inside. "Hello?"

The clock said it was after five. The volunteers would have left by now. Keith walked down the hill. The wooden bar for the flight barn door lay on the ground. When he checked the carport by Jenna's cottage, her Subaru was gone. A chill blanketed Keith's skin. Given all that had happened, Jenna wouldn't take off and leave doors unlocked.

An owl on a tether came around the corner. The bird flapped its wings, but didn't take off. Something was going on here. Jenna would never leave a bird out like that.

He gathered up the bird. As he headed toward the hill to put the bird in a cage, he spotted Jenna's car winding up a mountain.

Keith found a cage for the bird, raced outside and jumped in his truck. He ripped out of the parking lot and sped toward the mountain road, saying a prayer for Jenna's safety.

SIXTEEN

Jenna couldn't get a deep breath. She adjusted her sticky hands on the steering wheel. Peter turned toward her, pointing the gun at her.

She pressed her lips together. "What are you going to do?"

"This one will have to look like an accident."

What did he mean by *this one?* "Please, Peter." Her mouth felt dry. Even without the gun, Peter was strong. With the gun, she was completely outmatched.

"Course, you are always running over hill and dale to save those precious birds. It is entirely believable that sooner or later you might slip off a mountain."

Jenna's heart thudded against her rib cage. She had just passed the last crossroads. At this point, the road only went one place, to the top of Mount Larson. Unless they met a car coming down the mountain, her chances of finding help had gone from slim to none.

One thought tumbled over another as she tried to come up with possibilities for escape. There was nothing in the car she could defend herself with. A pocketknife wasn't much of a match against a gun.

"Why are you going so slow?" Each word was like a knife jab in her skin.

"This is a single lane dirt road with a hundred foot drop-off." The speedometer read fifteen. She probably could have pushed it up to twenty or twenty-five, but going slower gave her time to think.

Peter faced forward, but still pointed the gun toward her. In her peripheral vision, she saw him reach down and tug on the seat belt as though it were uncomfortable.

She needed to buy some time. Maybe if she got him talking. "So all your talk about caring about the birds was just a big front?"

"What I care about is the game," he said.

She fought to keep her voice level. The one thing she had control over was her emotions. Letting him see her sense of betrayal would give him the upper hand in an even greater way. "The game? What are you talking about?"

"The challenge of the hunt. At some point, shooting an elk through the head at one hundred yards with a permit in your pocket doesn't give you the rush you crave."

Jenna swallowed the rising anger. This man had totally deceived her. Her teeth clenched. She couldn't say anything without revealing her rage. The car descended into the final dip before the road would end at the edge of a cliff.

"Fortunately, I found a group of men who felt the same way and were willing to pay for the thrill." Peter's chin jerked up in a show of pride.

Jenna squeezed the steering wheel. Her knuckles turned white. She couldn't contain her anger any longer. "Most hunters have respect for the landowners, for the land and for what they hunt."

Peter leaned toward her, placing the gun on her temple. "Don't go getting all self-righteous on me." He spat his words out.

The pressure of the barrel of the gun made her eyes water. Her throat constricted. She forced out her words anyway. "I have to say it." She spoke through gritted teeth. "You sir, are a hunter without honor."

Peter huffed. "Honor? Give me a break." He gave the gun a final push against her temple before pulling it away.

They reached the flat area at the top of the mountain. Jenna brought the car to a stop.

"You stay right there," Peter said as the gun jerked in his hand, "until I come around and open your door."

Jenna pulled her hands off the steering wheel. Her gaze traveled to the rearview mirror. Fifty yards behind her was the edge of the forest. Could she get to the cover of the trees fast enough? Probably not. Given his shooting abilities, he could put a bullet in her before she had run ten yards.

Her fingers hovered by the keys still in the ignition. Maybe she could get turned around and down the mountain before he had time to shoot. Her trembling fingers touched the key.

She saw a flash of movement in her rearview mirror as Peter passed around the back of the car. She sat up straight. He jerked the door open and grabbed her shirt at the shoulder.

"Go to the rear of your car and grab one of those empty cages."

Jenna scanned the area around her as she made her way to the hatch and opened it. Her hand touched the smaller carrier.

"Take a bigger one," Peter commanded. "Lots of eagle nests around here. We want it to look like you were trying to rescue one of your precious goldens, and in your enthusiasm, you fell to your death."

"You never cared about the birds."

"Of course not, it was just a front so no one would suspect me." He flashed a grin that made her blood run cold.

Jenna's pulse drummed in her ears. She closed her eyes, unable to think of a coherent prayer. Only two words came to mind.

Please, God.

Peter leaned toward her and grabbed her phone off her belt. "Now go over to the edge of the cliff and throw the carrier off."

Her own heartbeat sounded like a death march playing in her head. Jenna bit her lower lip. Her feet felt like they were encased in cement.

"Go," Peter barked.

Jenna walked to the edge of the cliff. The initial drop off was a gradual forty-five degrees of rocks. She and Keith had climbed this mountain; there were ledges and footholds, but for the most part, it was a straight down.

Jenna tossed the carrier across the broken shale. It bounced once and rolled toward the edge. Peter threw her phone in the same direction, which bounced off several rocks before coming to rest a few feet from the carrier. It was pretty clear what the next part of his plan was. Would he push her or make her jump?

Jenna stalked over to him. "You haven't thought this through. You can't take my car. You'll have to hike off this mountain. I wouldn't have walked all the way up here to get a bird."

He leaned toward her, pushing the gun against her stomach and standing so close that his spit hit her face. He waved his own phone at her. "I'll get a ride from one of my many hunter buddies who are sworn to silence and have a little more loyalty than Eddie Helms."

"So you did shoot him?"

"Quit stalling." He slapped her hard across the jaw.

The stinging on her face became a tingle. She touched her finger to her cheek. Tears welled.

He pointed toward the rocks. His voice was a low, husky whisper. "You know what you have to do now."

"If you shoot me, they will trace the bullet and know you were involved."

Rage exploded in his eyes. "Turn around and walk."

"I won't. You'll have to shoot me." Either way, she was going to die. She had no intention of Peter Hickman getting away with this.

His upper lip rippled. He spun her around and poked the gun in her back. "Walk."

"Shoot me."

The pressure of the gun against her spine lessened. Peter stepped away from her and then ran to the car. He glanced at her and then down the mountain. He grabbed something from the rear of the car and stalked toward her.

"Change of plans." He glanced back down the road.

Jenna tried to turn to see what he saw, but he spun her around so she faced the cliff.

In his hand, he held the leather rope she used to tether birds and the cloth she threw on them to calm them. He had also grabbed a long rope she kept in the car. He tied her hands together.

"What's going on?"

"You ask too many questions." He placed the blindfold over her eyes.

Only a sliver of light snuck in at the bottom of the cloth. "If they find me like this, it won't look like an accident."

"I'll deal with you later. Now walk." He pushed on her back. The hard metal of gun bruised her spine.

Why had Peter changed his plan? Jenna took a hesitant step forward, testing the ground in front of her. Solid.

Peter pushed on her back again. "Hurry."

Something had panicked him. She could hear it in his voice.

She took several more slow steps.

"You've got a good twenty yards. Come on, run."

She obeyed. She was breathless by the time he yelled "Stop." A second later he came up to her and tied the rope around her waist. She pulled away, resisted, but he cinched the rope tighter, causing it to dig into her stomach.

He spoke into her ear. "I'm going to lower you down. Any lack of cooperation from you, and you risk tumbling off this mountain and breaking into a million pieces."

Her own sense of self-preservation kept her from fighting when she slipped off the cliff face and he lowered her. Her head grazed against the side of the cliff as rocks crashed into each other and cascaded down the mountain.

His voice came from above her. "Hold very still."

Her feet touched solid surface. She crumpled to her knees. The wind brushed against her face. She detected the rush of a distant waterfall, reminding her that she was close to Eagle Falls where so many eagles nested.

She could barely make out the mechanical

clang and hum of her car starting. The faint engine noises faded into the distance. Why on earth was Peter headed back down the mountain? Hope budded anew. Someone must be coming up the road.

Jenna inched her foot across the hard surface until she felt the drop off. If she moved, she would fall hundreds of feet.

SEVENTEEN

Keith was relieved to see Jenna's car parked at the last intersection before the road wound up the mountain. Maybe she had been called out on a big emergency, and she hadn't had time to lock the center.

He parked his truck beside her vehicle. No one was behind the wheel and the hatch was opened. Keith jumped out and circled the car. There were no carriers in the back. Jenna always had a small carrier and a large carrier with her. He studied the borders of the forest. The evergreens blended into dark shadows.

She wouldn't release a bird in such a thick forest anyway. It was usually easier to let them go in an open area or from a high place. He sauntered a few yards up the road. Wind blew through the grass of the meadow. He called her name. Fear crept into his awareness.

Something felt wrong.

A moment later, a man emerged from the trees holding one of the carriers. Maybe a volunteer. He wore a cowboy hat and dark glasses. The man shouted and waved. He drew closer.

Keith's stomach knotted. Peter Hickman.

Keith closed the distance between them. His feet pounded the hard earth. "Where is Jenna?"

Peter pulled off his sunglasses. "I imagine she is back at the center." He lifted the pet carrier. "I offered to help out with the release of a bird. She said I could take her car because it has all the needed equipment."

"You lie." Keith's blood boiled.

Peter took a step back and held up a hand. "Now hold on, just a minute."

Keith's hands curled into fists. He wanted to strangle this man. "Where. Is. Jenna?"

Peter stepped back again. "What is your problem? Calm down. I told you. She loaned me her car. Why don't you head to the center? I'm sure she is there."

"I was just there," Keith replied through clenched teeth. "The place was empty." Keith's heart pounded as adrenaline raged through him. Peter didn't know that Keith had linked him to the extreme hunters. Jenna was in danger. He knew it. Had Peter dragged her into the forest?

"Maybe she just stepped out." Peter offered Keith a crooked smile. "I've got to take the car back to the center. Are we good here?" His voice was patronizing.

Keith's mind reeled. Jenna must have made the same connections he had and now Peter had done something to her. "Where is she?" Keith lunged, hitting Peter across the jaw with a right hook. When Peter got back to his feet, he had a gun in his hand.

Keith swallowed hard to quell the storm brewing inside him. If Peter put the gun away, he might be able to jump him. If he played it cool, Peter might let his guard down. He struggled to keep the emotion out of his voice. "You're right. I should calm down. I'm sorry I got so upset." Each beat of his heart was a tick on the clock.

Jenna, where are you? What has he done with you?

Peter continued to hold the gun on him. "You kind of scared me." He circled around Keith without turning his back.

A few seconds more and Peter would be in the car and gone. He stepped toward the driver's seat, edging along the front bumper, still not taking his eyes off Keith.

Wild drums beat inside Keith's head. He could

not let this man go. Peter knew that Keith was on to him. He had the resources to be out of the country within hours. And Jenna?

Uncontrollable rage and desperation made Keith leap across the space between the two men and tackle Peter. A gunshot reverberated through the forest.

Jenna pressed close to the wall of the cliff. A branch brushed across her cheek. In the rush, Peter had not tied the blindfold very tight. She dipped her head so the branch hooked on the fabric. The branch was a centimeter from her eye. She leaned her head back, and the blindfold released from her eyes. The action caused her shoulder to brush against the loose rock of the cliff. A stone fell at her feet.

As the blindfold fell around her neck, she blinked. The ledge was even smaller than she had imagined. The view made her dizzy. Looking down only fueled her fear of heights.

Her arms strained from being tied behind her back. She tilted her head up. Peter had lowered her a good ten feet. The rope around her waist had been secured above her. A chill ran down her spine. Peter had said he wanted her death to look like an accident. He intended to come back for her.

He'd seen something down the mountain that had panicked him. Another car headed up this way, perhaps. But not Keith. Keith was on his way out of town. He was miles from here. Yet, he was the first person that came to mind. How many thousands of miles and how much time would there have to be between them before the strong connection died? She had to force herself to let it go. Just because he had rescued her so much in the past, saved her bacon in rivers and on the side of cliffs didn't mean he was good for her. He had saved her a thousand times from physical jeopardy but protecting her heart was a different thing altogether.

As much as she could without moving her legs, Jenna peered at the cliff face. She lifted her head. An eagle soared through the sky. The huge wingspan which always made her awestruck was the first clue that it was an eagle. As the bird drew closer, she could distinguish the white head of a mature baldy.

A hundred yards away and below her, the bird came in for a landing in a nest. The brown eaglet blended with the colors of the nest, but she could see slight movement. That guy needed to be pushed out of the nest and soon. This late in the summer most of the juveniles were out on their own. The older eagle flapped its wings before settling over her baby as the wind picked up.

What a picture of security.

Jenna held her breath as pieces of a psalm floated back into her head. Something about God protecting her with his wings. People, even good people like Keith, might let her down. Trusting in God was where the real safety in this world was. Her heart ached and she regretted her harsh words to Keith…and now it was too late.

The wind picked up even more. Her legs were starting to feel numb. She prayed. This was not the end. She was not without hope. Peter had seen someone coming up the mountain. They might get here before Peter could stop them. She was not about to give in to despair. She would do everything she could think of to get out of here.

She lifted her head as high as she could and shouted, "Hey, hey, somebody. I am down here."

Her foot slipped on the edge of the ledge.

Keith's body shuddered from the impact of falling on Peter. The two men rolled on the ground. Peter righted himself and subdued Keith by pinning his arm behind his back. The gun must have gone off. He saw Peter's hat and the crushed sunglasses but no gun.

Out of breath from the struggle, Keith wiggled to break free. "What have you done with Jenna?"

Peter didn't answer. He must be looking around for the gun. He released all the pressure off Keith's arm. Keith scrambled to his feet to see that Peter was pointing the gun at him again.

Behind him, Keith saw Jet racing through the tall grass. By the time Peter was aware of the noise, the dog had leaped up and grabbed Peter's shirttail. The attack was enough to throw Peter off balance, the gun fell out of his hand as he struggled to stay on his feet.

Keith scrambled for the gun and pointed it at Peter. Jet backed off but continued to bark, showing his teeth.

"Good boy, Jet." Keith tossed his cell phone to Peter. "Call the Sheriff."

With a wary glance toward Jet who released a low growl, Peter shook his head. "I haven't done anything wrong."

"We've linked you with the extreme hunters. No doubt you are the one setting things up. I am sure if we get some searchers out on your property, we can find that helicopter."

Peter's face blanched, and he took a step back.

Keith's head jerked up. "Now call the sheriff." He took in a breath. "And then...and then, tell me where Jenna is." His voice faltered. His thoughts jumbled. Was she still alive? What if Peter had done something to Jenna at the center and then hidden her somewhere? That didn't make sense. Why take her car and make himself look suspicious. "She is around here, isn't she? Tell me where she is."

Jenna's throat hurt from shouting. She pressed hard against the cliff face to keep from slipping again. She couldn't tell if the rope Peter had tied around her waist would hold her or not. Her legs had gone completely numb. She really needed to stretch out. The rope dug into her wrists and stomach.

She shifted slightly and more pebbles and dirt cascaded down the mountain. Slowly, carefully, she rose to her feet. Her legs tingled from lack of circulation. The view around her started to spin. She closed her eyes as a wave of despair washed through her. What if she died here? If she tumbled off this mountain, would the authorities even know Peter had done this?

Even as she was ready to give up, she heard

that still small voice that told her to try one more time.

Her throat felt like someone had run sandpaper over it. Jenna gathered her remaining energy, lifted her head and shouted. "Hey, somebody! I'm down here!"

She thought she heard something. A humming noise like a car motor? She shook her head. Was she just so desperate that now she was imagining sounds?

She cried out again. The faint sound of a dog barking reached her ears. Mustering strength, she lifted her head and shouted again. "I'm here!"

A strong clear voice responded. "Jenna!"

Her heart burst with joy. Keith had found her. "Down here."

His head materialized above her and then Jet's head appeared. The dog offered a sympathetic whine for her predicament. "You seem to have gotten yourself into a pickle."

She uttered a strange sound that was meant to be the words *thank God,* but the power of the rush of emotion through her made her words come out garbled.

Keith knelt. "You have no idea how glad I am to see you, Jenna Murphy." His face glowed with affection.

"You came back."

"I never left," he said.

Was that because of her or some other reason? "My hands are tied."

"I see that." He angled his head side to side, assessing further. "Hold on, I think we can get you out of there."

Keith disappeared and returned a few minutes later. He tossed a rope so it hung beside where she was. "I'm coming down to you."

"Where did you get the climbing gear?"

"After we talked about climbing again, I bought some gear and threw it in my truck." He buckled himself into the harness. "The sheriff is here to help. Peter is handcuffed in the car."

Keith rappelled down the mountain until he lined up with Jenna. Her back was to him. "Hold still. I'll cut the ties on your hands."

The pressure of the knife pressed against the rope. Her hands released, and she grabbed the rope tied around her waist as she wobbled backward. "Is this secure?"

Keith nodded. "This rope is not the best setup, but I'll help you. Come on, take your first foothold."

Her head buzzed and her pulse accelerated.

Keith positioned a hand on the middle of her back warming her to the core. The fogginess in her head cleared. If Keith was here, she wasn't afraid of falling.

"Like old times." She placed her foot on the tiny ledge.

"It would be nice if it was like old times for all time," Keith said.

Jenna reached up and found a handhold. Her foot searched for a ledge, and she pushed herself up. What was Keith saying? She bent her head to look down. "For all time? Are you serious?"

Her foothold gave way, and she slipped back down the rope to face Keith. They swung slightly, both of them hanging from their ropes. Keith angled his body, so he could rest his open palm on her cheek.

Jenna stared into the gentle gray eyes.

"For all time, for the rest of my life, with you," he whispered.

Keith wrapped the blanket the sheriff had given them tighter around Jenna's shoulders. The hard bench in the sheriff's office pressed against her back.

He leaned close to Jenna. "Are you okay?"

She nodded. She hadn't spoken much since they had gotten off the cliff face. He had proposed to her. What was her answer?

The sheriff clicked through pages on his

computer. "If you folks will just wait a few minutes more, I will take your statements."

The deputy had already taken Peter Hickman into a holding cell.

The sheriff tapped his keyboard. "You'll be glad to know that we matched the bullet in the eagle to the bullet in Eddie Helms. We've got a warrant to search Hickman's place to find the rifle."

"I thought Craig Smith had something to do with all this?" Jenna said.

"We questioned Craig earlier today. He did get into a card game with Eddie. Eddie was trying to wrap up loose ends before he blew the whistle. He was on his way out to pay off his debt to Craig."

The sheriff walked over to the other side of the room to retrieve documents. The deputy returned. After speaking to the sheriff, he sauntered over to Jenna and Keith.

"Sheriff wants me to take your statements." The deputy sat at his computer.

"I'll go first." Keith pulled his arm away from Jenna.

Keith went through the deputy's questions. Jenna did the same thing. They walked out into the cool of the evening. A few people sauntered along the sidewalks. Lights from the steak house glowed as people stepped inside.

"Do you remember what I said to you on the mountain?" Keith wrapped his arm around Jenna.

This was it. Her heart raced. "Yes, I remember."

"To be together like old times…for all time. Is that something you'd want?"

She stopped. Her gaze traveled to the library. All the lights had been turned off and shadows covered the steps.

He placed a hand on her shoulder. "I know that he wants to patch things up."

"I miss him." Jenna shook her head. "But letting him back into my life means he could hurt me again."

"I can't promise you that he won't relapse. I can tell you he is serious about staying sober."

"You haven't had a drink in twelve years." She walked ahead of him a few steps.

"Everyone's recovery is different."

She turned back around to face him. "I will try."

"I do think it is worth it, risking the hurt." He placed his hands on her shoulders and brought her closer. "When I thought Peter had done something to you…I saw my life without you and that was more unbearable than any hurt you may have caused me in the past."

Her lips parted. She tilted her head, eyes searching. "I'll risk it if you'll risk it."

"Like old times for all time?" He looked at her, his expression filled with expectation.

"No, better than old times. No more secrets."

"I'll take that as a yes then." He gathered her into his arms and kissed her.

EPILOGUE

Jenna's stomach fluttered more than the wings of the doves her father would release during the wedding ceremony.

"Jenna, are you ready to go?" Her father stood at the door to the tent that had been set up as a changing room for the bride and bridesmaids.

Cassidy gave her a last hug. She stepped back and held Jenna's face in her hands. "You look beautiful. Now, I need to go find my escort down the aisle."

As Cassidy exited, her father stepped toward her. He looked handsome in his dress pants and white button-down shirt, but what she liked best was how clear and filled with love his eyes were. "Nervous?"

"A little. I'm glad you're here." He held out an elbow, and she wrapped her arm through his.

It was a short walk down the hill to the clearing in the forest where the wedding party had gathered. An acoustic guitar played the wedding march. The music swelled. Jenna took in a quick, sharp breath as the attendees turned to look at her. Her father patted her hand. Etta and Norm smiled at her from the first row.

Keith stood at the end of the aisle wearing jeans and a light blue button-down shirt. She smiled. He was dressed up for Montana. His expression brightened when he looked at her. Warmth spread through her from the top of her head to her toes.

As her father handed her over to Keith she heard him whisper, "Take care of her."

"I will," he mouthed, looking directly at Jenna as he gathered her hands in his.

As they said their vows, Jenna looked into Keith's eyes. She still saw some of the skinny, wild kid who could talk her into anything, but there was something deeper, more anchored there, too.

She loved the man Keith had become.

Jenna said the final words of her vows, "... and to a lifetime of love and adventure."

On either side of them two large cages were opened and six doves flew out and fluttered over them as the attendees applauded.

Overhead, Jenna thought she heard the plaintive cry of a red-tailed hawk.

* * * * *

Dear Reader,

Though I had seen eagles at a distance and been awestruck by them, it wasn't until I had a close encounter with an eagle that I really appreciated how magnificent they are. My husband talked me into climbing a butte on his family ranch to see an old eagle's nest that had been occupied when he was a kid growing up.

Turns out the eagles had moved back in. I got to the top of the butte expecting to see some sticks and twigs formed into a nest. Instead, we caught a female bald eagle by surprise. She flew up and away, coming within a few feet of us. I don't think my heart has ever beat so fast.

When I took my kids to hear the educational talks that our local raptor rescue center puts on, I got to meet a blind owl and an eagle with a six-foot wingspan. I carried the idea around for some time of having a character who saved birds of prey. I am so glad I had an opportunity to show the important work the raptor rescue people do through the character of Jenna.

Blessings,

QUESTIONS FOR DISCUSSION

1. Do you think Jenna was wise for being cautious about entering into a romantic relationship with Keith? What were some of the reasons why she was so cautious?

2. Why is Keith guarded about sharing details about his past with Jenna?

3. Jenna has a secret she has been keeping for years. What events finally help her break free of the secret?

4. What does Keith do to show that he has changed? For Jenna? For his grandparents?

5. Keith uses painting to work through his emotions. Do you have a creative outlet that helps you see your problems more clearly?

6. Do you know any soldiers like Keith who not only have to recover from the trauma of war but also have to reintegrate into civilian life? What steps does Keith take to make the transition?

7.   What role does Jet serve in Keith's recovery?

8.   What did you think of the Montana setting? What details do you remember best?

9.   Do you think you would like to have a job like Jenna's, rescuing birds of prey?

10. Both Jenna and Keith have to heal relationships: Jenna with her father and Keith with his grandparents. Did anything in their story remind you of something in your own life?

11. Jenna goes for almost a whole year communicating with her father only on a limited basis. Do you think time apart in a relationship that is strained is a good idea?

12. Jenna feels a special connection to her father because they both love to read. She and Keith formed a friendship based around outdoor activities. How have you built relationships with friends and family members?

13. What does Jenna do to make Keith realize she accepts him just as he is?

14. Do you think a friendship like the one Jenna and Keith had as kids was a good basis for a romantic relationship when they were older?

15. Have you ever had to deal with someone who had addiction issues? Were there events you felt you handled well and other choices you wish you could change? Did anything in Jenna's story strike a chord with you?